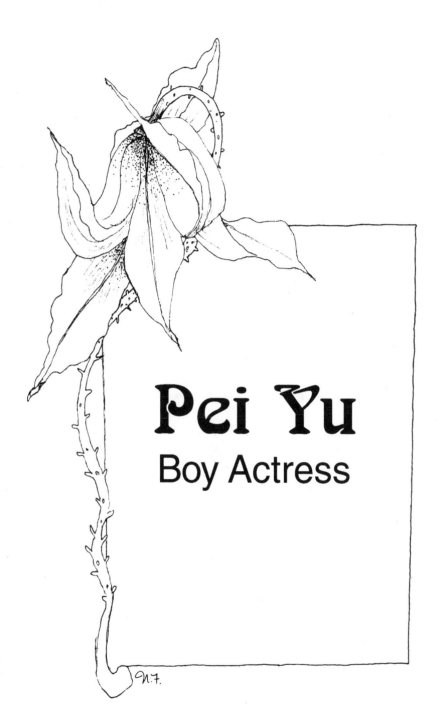

Pei Yu
Boy Actress

Nemi Frost

Pei Yu
Boy Actress

by George Soulié de Morant

translated from the French by
Gerald Fabian and Guy Wernham

illustrations by
Nemi Frost

Alamo Square Press
San Francisco

Twenty numbered copies of this book
have been hand-colored and embellished
by artist Nemi Frost.

Original French edition *Bijou-de-Ceinture* copyright © 1925, Flammarion, Paris

English Translation copyright © 1981, Gerald Fabian and Guy Wernham

Translator's Note, Author's Biography, Glossary copyright © 1991, Gerald Fabian

First Alamo Square Press edition, San Francisco, 1991

ISBN 0-9624751-3-0 (hard cover)
ISBN 0-9624751-4-9 (paperback)

LC 91-073943

10 9 8 7 6 5 4 3 2 1

Author's Introduction

This is not a purely imaginary account, a fairy tale, or an unlikely and exotic fantasy written to astonish the reader. Rather, it is the story of real lives and adventures to which I was witness.

Since childhood, I have seemed destined to devote myself to the arts, literature and theater. So naturally, from my earliest visits to China, I found myself drawn to the world of Chinese theater, a world of strange sentiments and still stranger actions. This is a world almost completely unknown and little understood by the Occident either at that time or today.

I felt as if the gloomy shroud of hypocritical repression and discontent that hangs heavily over Europe had been lifted and I had found again that free and healthy classical civilization which we glimpse in those Greek novels and poems that escaped the destructive attention of the puritanical barbarians.

When it came to the question of love in this revived world, no one ever saw women. Neither courtesans, matrons nor virgins appeared in social life whether at feasts, parties or cult festivities. Before the revolution of 1911, the only women seen in the streets were those of the servant class or those stripped by poverty of any other concern but that of staying alive.

At the theater women were not allowed on the stage or in the audience. At first my own eyes, forewarned as they were, could not get used to this absence of the opposite sex, which would have been fatal in Europe with the ridiculous cut of our male attire, its gloomy colors, its dismal fabrics. On the Chinese stage, at least, long hair and silken robes brought a certain spectacle, a certain grace and something of the unexpected to the audience.

It was not because of their deceptive feminine appearance and mannerisms, however, that the young actors were showered with amorous attentions at the banquets and *promenades galantes* they adorned with their presence. We were very far away from those imperfect imitations, those *décolleté* female impersonators that Montmartre tourists gawk at in a well-known night spot.

Rather, it was the Idea of Gracefulness itself that was admired; charm and seduction in their pure form; refinement, harmony of voice and of spirit; the art of giving joy with a look, a word or a gesture.

In this work I wanted to portray the souls of the actors, the souls that were of an often admirable nobility, yet always full of a passionate, moving, refined subtlety, as if molded and formed by the delicate poetry and the magnificent feelings of the characters they had personified from their earliest childhood.

I wanted to record here a few aspects of their recent past, which is already fading, before the moment when the last Europeans who knew them will also disappear and there will be no one left to attest to the veracity of my work in all its characters and episodes.

Pei Yu is a real person. Prince Li died in precisely the circumstances I have described. And it is with a sincere thought of homage and profound admiration for the moving heroism of the minister Yüan Ch'ang and of the censor Hsü Ch'ing Ch'êng that I allow myself to use their real names and to translate literally some passages from their memorials to the Throne and to describe their last moments.

G.S.M., 1925

Translator's Introduction

Guy Wernham, translator of Isidore Ducasse, Le Comte de Lautréamont's *Chants de Maldoror* for New Directions, was living in the old Montgomery Block of San Francisco, the grand and historic Greek Revival hotel that stood where the Transamerica Pyramid now stands, at the corner of Washington and Montgomery streets. In the late '50s, I had just returned from Mexico when Guy handed me a curious little novel written in French about a Chinese boy opera star by an author completely unknown to me, George Soulié de Morant.

Guy said, "Jerry, you ought to translate this!" I read it, and was stupefied, not to say taken aback. I reacted in an alarmingly conservative manner. I was shocked by the frankness of the work. I don't recall if I had read Genet at that time or not. Years went by swiftly. In 1960, I returned to U.C. Berkeley to take a degree in French Literature and Romance languages. In 1962, Guy Wernham who had been in decline for some years, vanished from the scene. Some six years later, I was frantically rummaging through my shelves trying to find something good to translate, when suddenly *Bijou-de-Ceinture* fell out onto the floor. I picked it up enthusiastically. I translated two chapters for a lark. I had now completely revised my opinion of the previous decade. The piece now seemed a rare and exotic adventure. Unintelligible before, it now sprang to life.

I took my chapters to a writer's workshop that spring. They were not well received. Something in my style, a few ill-chosen phrases, provoked general hilarity. But fate did not let me off there. Within two weeks I met Michael Wernham, Guy's only son, who had just returned from Paris. I mentioned that I was currently translating some chapters of the work as his father had once suggested. He said, "Oh yes. *Bijou-de-Ceinture*. Guy was translating it himself when he died." I became excited. Within moments Michael had not only offered me use of his father's manuscript, but offered to waive all rights in my favor. I immediately set to the task.

Over the next few years there were large interruptions. I abandoned Berkeley for the East Coast, finally settling near Washington, D.C. In Washington, *Bijou-de-Ceinture* seemed to take hold of me, giving me no peace until the task was accomplished. Insomnia set in. Then suddenly, within the space of a year, all the chapters were finished. Re-writing and editing came next.

Luckily, the Library of Congress was at hand with its magnificent Department of Orientalia. It was a pleasure to work with the erudite and Mandarin-like staff, many of whom seemed to wear the air of dynasty wisdom and cultivation. I was able to find references and data for an entire glossary.

The next problem was finding George Soulié de Morant's son and literary heir. I had known since the '60s of his existence through the French *Who's Who (Qui est Qui)* but those titles, "Order of the Golden Dragon of Vietnam, etc." behind his name seemed formidable. Would he actually receive me? And where did he live? Only Flammarion (the original publishers) could tell me, and they were very slow in answering and most noncommittal.

All the while a benevolent fate had been impelling me towards the European continent and Paris, where I was able to confront Flammarion and receive direct answers.

Nevile was, in fact, very much alive. He and his wife lived in Neuilly. I called him with a certain amount of trepidation. What would be his attitude towards his father's letters? Had they been on good terms? Both imponderables. Nevile came on the line. Within moments I was reassured. He was in favor of bringing out everything that his father ever wrote. *Bijou-de-Ceinture* was singled out with especial affection!

Now my problem was that the manuscript was not at hand. I had stored it in Texas (of all places) before leaving Washington. Luckily, a party of friends, two of whom were Texans, planned to rendezvous with me in Barcelona toward the end of June. Would they bring the manuscript? Certainly. After a hilarious St. John's Eve in that ancient seaport, I hurried back to Paris and delivered the manuscript to Nevile. He pounced and bore it away for perusal while I set out for Reims, Trier, Hamburg and Copenhagen.

I returned to Paris at the end of August and went to work with

Nevile, going over every page of the text, carefully catching and amending errors. During this interval I had the opportunity to dine with Nevile frequently. In retrospect I find that I wish I'd had the presence of mind to tape his words. Amazing details about his father's life kept rising to the surface.

In addition to the splendid assistance in editing, Nevile's remarkable command of English made a flattering background to his praise and approval of the Wernham-Fabian translation, and also secured the backing of the Société des Gens de Lettres, which was obligatory under the terms imposed by his father's estate. The Société des Gens de Lettres, according to the *Oxford Companion to French Literature,* "founded in 1838 by Louis Desnoyers (1802-68, novelist and man of letters) with the support of the most prominent literary men of the period, is primarily an authors' rights society in matters of copyright, publication, etc."

Once back in America, finding a publisher for *Bijou-de-Ceinture* (now *Pei Yu: Boy Actress)* became another challenge. Most found it too purple, too odd, too this or too that. In 1990, I came across Bert Herrman of Alamo Square Press at a writer's conference in San Francisco. He found the same passion in the work that I had decades earlier and, with his associate Karen Schiller, worked with me to edit it and prepare it in its present form.

G.F., 1991

1

Basking in the crystal clear light of the winter sun filtering through the window panes of a lofty Peking pavilion, I allowed my gaze to drift toward the rosy mist of flowering peach trees. Their reflections danced on the waters of a lake girded by odd-shaped rocks. Farther on, my eyes were drawn to the golden spendor of the Imperial rooftops, fleetingly revealed among the slender, flesh-tinted branches of the city's tall trees.

But my attention never really strayed from the supple, natural grace of my friend Pei Yu, stretched out near me in an English armchair with mahogany stiffness that seemed the proper setting for more roughly masculine attitudes. The folds of his long, silken gown, brocaded with a pattern of midnight blue foliage, outlined the elegantly rounded softness of a body that seemed lacking in any bones. His hair, cut short in the latest fashion, shocked the senses, which would have chosen to see this face, with its enormous deep-set eyes and delicately chiseled features, framed in longer tresses.

The room where we dreamed was an exotic fantasy for Peking (for the Far East, London is exotic). The simplicity of the heavy, stark furniture reminded me of London's foggy skies and the fever of our blindly physical lives. It made me uncomfortable. My subconscious, trying to escape, allowed me to envision only images of long ago, and to recall the remotest memories I had of the famous actor.

Without doubt, half-reading my thoughts, he smiled and addressed me in that harmonious voice and musical elocution to which he owed his immense success.

"How many upheavals there have been in my life—and in the universe—since that time, scarcely twenty years ago, when you turned your compassionate glance towards the little slave I was at that time."

"Even then I saw in you the radiant dawn of your future glory," I responded politely.

He inclined his head in thanks and continued:

"Actually there has never before been a period in world history when all men and nations have undergone such radical metamorphoses. Your European annals tell how once you gave glory, titles and fortune to soldiers and courtesans, while artists were only hirelings. Then, scarcely half a century ago, you turned your attentions and rewards to literary lights, painters and actors. Now our daily press tells us that the man who made the largest sum of money last year throughout the Occident was a pugilist, a formerly penniless black prizefighter, if I am not mistaken. In China before the 1911 Revolution everything went to courtesans and high officials. Today we are in the age through which you have already passed: the artist is surrounded with an aura of admiration and wealth. Will we be able to avoid the day when prizefighters get everything?"

While listening to him I struck a match on a box decorated with Japanese motifs and waited for it to flame so that I could light my cigaret of Fukien tobacco.

But my subconscious, suddenly abandoning time and space, took a leap backward to that day in the distant past when I met Pei Yu for the first time.

Once more I peered through the rosy and pearl-gray light of a late-autumn dawn, to a broad expanse of rippling water with thickly growing reeds that yielded to low banks sparsely planted with willows. Toward the north, above a high, black, notched battlement, towered a glazed-brick pagoda already glittering under the dappled caresses of the rising sun.

I was on the high afterdeck of a mighty junk, leaning against a richly carved bulwark, watching the arrival of a dozen or so small, wretchedly dressed boys, each carrying his skimpy bundle, hurrying along together beneath the eye of a rather unsavory-looking gentleman.

Was it a boarding school? But nothing in the appearance of the man reminded me of the bespectacled and worthy deportment of a schoolmaster. The little ones, giggling and tumbling over one another, were behaving with a good deal more license than is usual for school children.

One of them sensed my stare and raised his head. He had a thin, sweet face with eyes deep-set and large, to which the clear light of day gave a violet tinge, a too-serious mien. . . Borne along by the press of the crowd, he disappeared into the junk.

From Nanking, I was going to take a new diplomatic post in the North, and I had elected to follow the Imperial Canal to Peking in the hope of encountering unfamiliar scenes and characters over which occidental life had not yet thrown its winding sheet of banality. For this same reason, instead of chartering a private vessel, I had engaged a cabin in one of those great junks which once were the only means of transportation for both passengers and cargo alike between the two cities. My stateroom with its balcony astern had retained traces of its former splendor—carved bulkheads lacquered with gold over purple, ornate mirrors, and windows with translucent paper panes stretched over a trellis of elegant foliage patterns.

We had put ashore at some distance from the city of Yangchow in order to avoid the costly vexations of the city toll, which made European customs inspections, however maddening, seem pleasant. It was there that this group of children came on board amid the crowds of travelers and their servants, and the shouts of the crew stowing away cargo and the last of the baggage before casting off the hawsers and hauling in the gangways.

Hoisting her lofty, narrow, ochre-tinted sail, the antique vessel glided through serene waters, at first skirting the town's somber walls, then venturing into the vast flood plain of fertile countryside, all blue and rose beneath the crystalline morning radiance.

A deep silence had followed the violent activity of casting off. A few water birds, disturbed by our approach, flew off uttering raucous cries. All human habitation had vanished.

Into the midst of this primeval, intoxicating peace, burst suddenly the piercing, pure, clear notes of a strange melody sung by a voice so intense and so high that it seemed to be emitted from the zenith into the icy blue, and I was impelled to glance toward the sky, until reason recalled my attention to the junk's bridge.

There, seated cross-legged on the deck, was the pale, dark-eyed child who had come aboard at dawn. He was singing, his head uplifted. Beside him, two other little boys dressed in rags sat in the same position, listening. Before him was the suspicious-looking man balancing on his bent knee a two-stringed violin with a resonance chamber made from a length of bamboo, rendering sounds like a pipe organ.

When the child had finished the man said curtly, "That's good! Hao!" Then another of the boys took up the same tune. But his shrill voice and incessant mistakes provoked harsh criticism from the violinist. The "boarding school" was evidently a company of actors.

I took advantage of this temporary lull to ask the wide-eyed child the stock questions demanded of travelers who are following the same course. "Where are you going?" He nodded politely and answered, "We are headed for the capital."

"Which company will you sing with?"

"The Kuang-Tê-Pan, 'the Company of Increasing Virtue.'"

"Ah, yes!" I said. "Your theater is on the Ta-Chia-Lan."

"You are familiar with the capital?" he demanded enthusiastically.

We were interrupted. It was his turn to study another song. His master—the *shih fu*—sang it, bar by bar, stressing the downbeat. The child repeated it in his pure voice. Each passage was gone over. Finally the entire piece was sung almost perfectly.

The violinist's satisfaction was apparent. When the lesson was over and he got up, I slipped a piece of silver into his hand, complimenting him on his talent as a musician, and on his good fortune to have a pupil with the voice of a phoenix, lovelier than K'ang Ngo, the Moon Fairy.

"Pei Yu!" he exclaimed. "He's priceless, a treasure, a real *pao-pei*. My fortune is made . . . if someone doesn't steal him from me. But I watch over him night and day. Look, I even bought one of your handguns in Shanghai!" And he produced a heavy revolver from the folds of his robe. Then, doubtless flattered by the attention of a "foreign devil," he introduced himself as "Master Chang" and chattered away unreservedly, confiding many things to me about his pupils, winding up with:

"When we get to Peking, since you like Pei Yu, you may call for him whenever you wish. I'll always send him to you."

So it was that I first met Pei Yu. Later on, through the reports of some and the malicious gossip of others, I became informed of the smallest details of his childhood.

3

Pei Yu was born in one of those little aggregations of humans lost within that immense plain forming the whole of North China. During the winter it is an unchanging desert; as far as the bluish horizon, nothing varies the monotony of the naked plains where the wind raises whirlwinds of khaki-colored dust.

At long intervals there comes into view what seems at first to be a small wood, but which on closer inspection is revealed to be a group of low-built houses with yellowish clay-block walls and gray tiled roofs overgrown with flowering weeds. The houses, surrounded by ditches, cringe half-hidden under a lattice of slender, bare-branched willows.

This is a country without mystery, where everything approaching can be viewed from as far away as the eye can see, where any desire to leave is crushed by the certainty of never being able to reach any other place, where the unexpected retreats into the domain of the improbable. Over the thousands of years that men have succeeded men on these plains, thought and action have remained the same from generation to generation.

Vastness, immutability, suppression of time and space. Impassiveness and indifference to all things. Under such conditions, why make any effort at all? Would it not be wiser to follow Lao Tzu's advice and make a home here, forgotten by all, while determinedly practicing the theory of No Action? At least one might achieve eternity through anticipated death, for what are they who live thus, if not in a sense already dead?

Pei Yu recalled everything from the moment of his birth, down to the smallest details, since nothing changed. For at each birth he attended he heard the same invariable words: exclamations of joy and felicitations if the newborn were a boy; condolences if it were a girl. Since it was assumed that women could neither work like men nor carry forth sacrifices to the ancestors, they were useful only for breeding.

The child soon began to help his parents cultivate their modest fields and to care for the chickens and the ducks. His principal job consisted of gathering slender twigs, straws—anything that could be used to feed the hearth fire of the *k'ang*, that wide, low bed of brickwork on which the entire family lives and sleeps.

No wayfarer ever passed their village. None of their number had ever visited the city. They were unaware of the outside world, and the outside world knew nothing of their existence. Peasants lost on this limitless plain, they could easily recite the most ancient poem in Chinese literature, which their ancestors on this same plain had sung centuries before:

> At sunrise, I work.
> At sunset, I rest.
> I drink from the well that I have dug.
> I eat from the field which I till.
> Of what use to me the Emperor's might?

The Emperor's might descended upon such a man only once a year, after the harvest at the beginning of winter, when a tax collector from the governor arrived with a detachment of cavalry to levy taxes. The villagers wailed and protested, but under the menace of corporal punishment they always paid up.

One day the tax collector arrived with only two men. So the villagers, pretending to listen, ganged up on them, seized them and quietly strangled them. The bodies were buried at once in an abandoned field. The money they found was shared among the participants. When an inquiry was opened, the villagers of the entire region insisted unanimously that they had paid their tax. A verdict was reached that the collector had embezzled his take and the incident was closed.

Since the village was too poor to fill a priest's useless mouth, there was no temple. There was also no school; a few well-meaning ancients instructed the children in such sparse elements of writing and history as they themselves had fortuitously picked up during their own lives.

Appalled by the image of such an existence, I once asked Pei Yu whether no one ever wearied of living so, if no one ever dreamed of leaving, of seeking his fortune. Completely astonished, he replied:

"What for? We were happy. We always had a year's supply of grain stored away in case of a bad harvest. We knew nothing of sickness, or even boredom, for there was always work in the fields to be done. We were rich and happy, since all our needs were satisfied, and we never heard of anyone living in any other manner."

Everything in their souls was natural, simple and necessary. Observing the seasons, animals and their neighbors gave them clear-cut, indisputable information which was exactly what they needed day by day. No fallacious arguments from orators or divines ever came to upset the flawless interplay of their reason.

Pei Yu was still quite small when, playing one day in the hot sunshine, he caught sight of his 12-year-old cousin standing against a section of wall in the rear of one of the houses vacated by the field workers.

Pei Yu approached him full of curiosity. The cousin, blushing, let him examine fully the tumescent object of his amazement and, in turn, drew aside Pei Yu's garment. How could one describe what he saw? A pale, scarcely opened *fleur-de-lis* would have had more firmness. O, what humiliation! Pei Yu would remember all his life the feelings of that moment. In this way the sacred instinct which nature gives us with life, the source of all our actions, the supreme motive for living was awakened in Pei Yu.

After this, the two cousins became inseparable. Whenever they could find a moment alone, they hastened to compare what they called their "talismans," their "tortoise heads," and they played with them in a hundred different ways.

But there came a day when Pei Yu, having played longer than usual with his cousin's "jade stem," was surprised to see him tremble and falter. A glance assured him—without enlightening him—that his cousin did not seem to be in pain. What ailed him?

Laughter from behind caused Pei Yu to turn his head. His own father was standing there—probably had been watching them for some time. He sat down beside them and sent the smaller boy to fetch his pipe, which he said he had left in the house.

At first Pei Yu took off trustingly. But his observant mind had noticed a certain gleam in the farmer's eye. He became suspicious of a trick to get rid of him and, perhaps motivated by jealousy, concealed himself behind a haystack nearby.

From then on he saw no more of the other boy, whom his father kept dragging off to secret hideouts. Besides, the cousin now visibly disdained his little companion and manifestly preferred the new games to their puerile tricks.

The poet Wang Hsun (*circa* 1650) sings of the innocent upsets of early youth in a still celebrated poem:

> Almost thirteen,
> While studying hard
> Your after-palace flower
> > gets plucked!
>
> Suddenly,
> > fifteen,
> Spring comes on—
> You gaze after beauties
> And
> > their glossy kingfisher jewels.

When
            the robe flies open,
The darling elf espied,
You boast of
Having known the famous Empress
                              Chao Fei-yen.

Then up goes the back-hair
And you are unseated,
            unhorsed like the
                        King of Liang.

In succession you sing: wild swans, storks, moonlit
                        clouds that scud—stately
                        saraband, jasmine flowers and
                        dawn's reflections on a lake.

On your solitary pillow
You dream of rising
Up through scented vapors
            to the bewitching hill

Only, you have to satisfy yourself
By watching servant girls
Who steal away
                        alone.

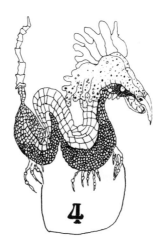

Mostly idle from then on, Pei Yu one day joined three of his playmates who, squatting on the ground, copied some ideograms in the dust with sticks that an almost bald, white-haired septuagenarian traced with his cane on the deserted threshing floor.

The child's beautiful eyes attracted the old man's attention. Immediately, with an admiring indulgence, he began to praise the first outlines sketched by the beginner's twig. That very evening he proposed to Pei Yu's father that the boy take private lessons for a *chin* of rice per month. He waxed lyrical with promises of an education sufficient to qualify the child for the highest posts in the state.

The father hesitated. Everyone knows what his neighbor's word is worth, but a *chin* of rice has real value. On the other hand, suppose that by chance the teacher was not lying? The mother's enthusiasm made up his mind for him. The child began to take private lessons each day, in the sun beside a haystack that protected them from the cold wind.

The old man was so overflowing with kindness and caresses that Pei Yu soon lost all his shyness. He grew so confident that, forgetting caution, he found himself asking the meaning of the last episode of his adventures with his young cousin.

Old men in all countries have a passionate love of youth. As their potency decreases, one could almost say that their desire increases to test their strength against greater and greater challenges. Easy victory, shallow triumph.

In this connection, I shall always remember the answer given by a young mother I interviewed at the hospital of a remote town where I was trying to help out the overburdened head doctor as best I could.

She held in her arms a child barely 18 months old, and she turned the infant over so that I could see telltale lesions and the scar tissue of what is known in those parts as the "flower sickness." I asked indignantly who had dared to treat the child so brutally. Wide-eyed with astonishment at my ignorance, she replied, "Why his grandfather, naturally."

Pei Yu's confidences broke down his teacher's last reserve and the old man told himself the long-awaited moment had finally arrived. Despite his senility he pushed things a bit too far, and the neophyte began to cry. The more the child struggled, the more the old man intensified his efforts.

Finally released from the old man's grasp, the toddler, weeping bitterly, ran to complain to his father, who began to laugh, quoting a passage from a well-known romance: "Virtuous men have about as many monuments raised in their honor as do widows faithful to the memory of dead husbands."

But a few days later when the teacher came to ask for his rice, Pei Yu's father answered that the quantity had been exactly what he had had to sell in order to buy some soothing ointment for the pupil.

This idyllic period did not last very long, for at about the same time an official agent, arriving to collect taxes, informed the assembled villagers that according to a proclamation of the new governor, the August Emperor in His profound Wisdom had authorized His subjects to massacre all "foreign devils," the *yang kuei tzu*, who yearly came in greater numbers to settle along the coasts and in the large cities. When a total stranger forces his way into a house, one has a perfect right to kill him. Everyone approved this, and it was decided that they must kill all foreigners who strayed into those parts. Doubtless the booty would reward the effort.

But the old men, silent in the presence of the tax collector, shook their heads after his departure, saying:

"Everything that assures us our livelihood comes from the soil and from our labors. The authorities give us nothing. They are forever trying to relieve us of our property. Our village is self-supporting, and we ask help from no one. Yet they insist on their taxes as if we owed them something. Indeed, if every time they tried to bleed us for more, we had not slaughtered the officials and burned down their palaces, we should long ago have been crushed by taxes. Believe us, everything the government tells us is only a lie invented to fleece us more thoroughly. If you do not instantly rise up and destroy the local authorities, you will all perish tomorrow."

Nobody believed them and in that all were mistaken. Indeed, with the support of the new governor, gangs of good-for-nothings, "floaters," took advantage of the situation under the pretext of hunting down aliens and those who practiced the immoral doctrines of the Occident. They raided the countryside to pillage, rape, murder and burn. The governor, heavily bribed and not daring to prosecute patriots, took pains not to have them arrested.

The boy's village was among the first to be attacked and razed, after putting up a losing defense.

Pei Yu, who was then 10 years old, was enraged to see his mother attacked by one of the vandals. The attacker dropped his weapon, a long poleaxe, in order to free his hands. The child, transported by his own fury, seized the razor-sharp lance. Holding it under one arm, while supporting it with two hands, he ran forward full force, just as he had sometimes done with his playmates when they used to tilt with one another using wooden poles in the haystacks. The blade, entering the stomach through the soft underbelly, plunged deeply in. Screaming hideously, the man fell to the floor while his executioner ran off to hide in the fields.

The next morning, after the bandits' departure, he came back to the smoking hovels. A few survivors were wandering among the ruins, including his former teacher. Since nothing edible remained, they left at once for the city. There the old man sold the child for five ounces of silver to the director of a theater company on tour.

When I asked Pei Yu if he had tried to run away, he replied:

"Why? I eat rather better now than ever in my life. I enjoy my work. I am not mistreated. What more could I ask?"

Meanwhile on the junk's afterdeck, music lessons and rehearsals of well-known operas went on day after day from morning "rice" to the last "rice" of evening. I soon became familiar with almost all of the troupe's repertory. My greatest pleasure was derived from hearing the *shih fu* improvise on the flute for an occasional opera in the *K'un-ch'iang* style, the most ancient of all, with its five-note scale, its sweet, harmonious tones and its libretti having to do almost always with exceptional and impassioned love.

Lulled as if in a dream by the persistent modulations of the melody, my mind followed the gist of the drama, while my eyes, straying out beyond the ragged actors, gazed into the infinite stretches of the vast landscape, aquatic and empty, which passed by as the junk moved slowly and soundlessly onward.

Sometimes they performed a work in the *Pang-tzu* style as one of the boys punctuated the solemn, deafening, almost cello-like notes of the big, double-choired *hu-hu* with the unruffled rattle of his *pang-tzu*. Then the boys would adopt the noble postures of ancient heroes and in their shrill voices uttter the pompous sentiments attributed by history the world over to its illustrious men.

But mainly they rehearsed female roles, for during this period women were not allowed on the stage. Pei Yu studied the attitudes of the *Chêng-tan*, the woman in love, and of the *Hua-chêng-tan*, the seductive courtesan, making more feminine his natural grace, each day aping more successfully the balanced walk of bound feet, modest or passionate glances, head and body movements that stirred the emotions of the spectator.

The role of the *ch'ou*, comical and crafty, came quite naturally to a thin, sly lad named Precious Treasure, whom nature seemed to have destined for the part by giving him small, sparkling eyes, an insolently snub nose, and thin and cynically playful lips.

The *ch'ou* hated Pei Yu with all the feverish violence of a gangrenous jealousy.

During one of the early days of our voyage, he deftly slipped some arsenic, which he undoubtedly purchased at Yangchow, into his charming colleague's tea cup. Luckily it was an overdose, and his intended victim had not been able to keep down the first mouthful.

Attracted by piercing shrieks and anguished pleas, I found the *ch'ou* in one corner of the bridge, his wrists bound to his ankles so as to expose naked thighs to the bamboo stick wielded with machine-like regularity by Master Chang. Twisting and squirming like a snake, the victim vainly sought to escape the blows. They were violent enough, but I noticed quickly that they fell each time in a different spot, and since the bamboo was not splintered into sharp-edged strips such as those used for the punishment of criminals, it would not break the skin and thus risk depreciating the boy's intrinsic value, but raised only welts that would pain him no longer than a month.

The rest of the passengers had formed a silent circle around them. Custom forbade interference in other people's affairs. A bystander apprised me of the facts.

When the punishment was over, curious to know how the culprit had been detected, I inquired of the *shih fu*, who was mopping his brow. He answered, shrugging:

"I was sure that he would try to kill his comrade, either with poison or by pushing him overboard. Since he had no knife, and Pei Yu was on his guard, it had to be poison. But how did he hide that arsenic? I frisked him and his baggage thoroughly. He's got to be more crafty than I figured."

"And did he confess?"

"Him! Only torture would tear a confession out of him. But I didn't need that. When Pei Yu threw up the poison his face was a dead-giveaway. It is easier to lie with one's tongue than with one's eyes."

"What frightful evil in that little creature!"

"Why all the surprise? He wants to be the star and does his best to eliminate rivals. That's natural enough. Now I'll be forced to keep Pei Yu at my side day and night, that's all."

Our junk, continuing to forge northward up the Imperial Canal, arrived one morning at a small port in Shantung. A teeming mob was milling about from the gray houses of town down to the waterfront. Our vessel encountered some difficulty in finding a place to dock, for there was a scarcity of spaces, and the only adequate one was occupied by a superb, gilded and sculptured double-decker beyond which we were finally able to rest.

Before us, one by one, arrived numerous green and blue palanquins with tin and copper ornaments sparkling in the sun. The bearers, escorts, jostling crowds of curious spectators and the guns firing off salutes made an impressive noise.

Over a hundred chief magistrates were soon assembled there in voluminous sable robes, their fur-trimmed caps topped by buttons of coral or sapphire from which were suspended bunches of two- or three-eyed peacock feathers, and triple or quadruple fox tails, their insignia of office.

According to gossip it was no less than an Imperial Envoy that all the authorities in the province were escorting with so much pomp. That was the omnipotent Prince of the Blood, Prince Li, delegated by the Emperor to conduct the annual sacrificial ceremonies on the Holy Mountain of the East, the *Tai Shan*.

Curiosity, naturally, had drawn us all to the railing to watch the procession pass our vessel. Why, amid that sea of faces, did Prince Li have to single out Pei Yu?

He saw the boy and stopped dead, forgetting to balance his shoulders in that posture of importance demanded by custom. Briefly he stared at the child, then turned and spoke rapidly to one of his companions, a Manchu of mien almost as grim and overbearing as the

Prince's own.

Chang the *shih fu* had observed the direction and expression of the Prince's gaze. He turned pale. Terror was depicted so vividly on his suddenly pinched face that I could not help asking him in a whisper what he was afraid of.

"Then you don't know of Prince Li? Everything he sees he wants. What he wants he takes. And whoever is rash enough to try to defend his belongings is beaten, robbed, killed. He has a choir of twenty singers picked up like that. He noticed Pei Yu. I'm ruined!"

Drops of cold sweat trickled down his forehead. Amazed by such abject terror, I exclaimed:

"If you fear him that much, why don't you clear out without waiting around? He can't do anything now, with all the officials in the province watching. Take off right away. Who will notice you in all this hubbub? By the time his men think to hold you, you'll be far away."

He stared at me blankly for a while. Then the light dawned on his face. He pressed two fists together and bowed deeply, saying with much emphasis:

"You have saved our lives! I will never forget this, nor shall Pei Yu . . . "

I had to break in and urge him to get ready. His preparations did not take long.

A few moments later the boys made their way through the crowd of passengers, leaping down upon the quay to be lost amid the jostling mass of sightseers. Pei Yu, having remained up to the last with his *shih fu*, now knelt before me. I raised him up immediately, while slipping a silver ingot into his sleeve. Then he too vanished into the moving waves of strollers.

There had not been a minute to lose. On the quay troops were brutally clearing out room among the spectators. Heavy green palanquins, each borne by eight porters, were lined up in readiness, awaiting the signal. The magistrates shook their clasped hands in the direction of the princely junk now shoving off from the quay. There was a final salvo. Then the sable robes bowed deeply to one another and, according to order of precedence, filed into the palanquins. Procession and escort disappeared. The quay was almost deserted.

From high up on the afterdeck I watched the maneuvers of the other junk, only half-believing the *shih fu*'s fears. It happened quite simply. As soon as the two vessels were alongside each other, grappling hooks were thrown out from the other junk and made fast to us.

Immediately a dozen ruffians wearing dark blue turbans boarded us and swarmed over our bridge like tigers or wolves, to use a popular image. They spread out all over the ship, forcing open cabin doors and doubtless laying rude hands on anyone who offered any resistance.

I overheard them questioning crew and passengers and could not disguise my amusement at their discomfiture when they reappeared with hangdog looks and climbed back over the side to confront their master. Prince Li was evidently furious, for I heard yells of rage coming from the main cabin, followed soon by pleas and howls.

Then the grappling hooks were detached and the vessel got under way. When it was at a safe distance, a medley of curses and insults arose from our cabins, evidence that the vandals had not completely wasted their time.

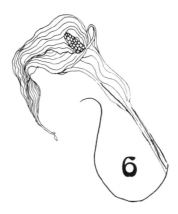

6

Once I arrived in Peking, business cares absorbed all my time and energies. I would never have thought about the details of my trip if I had not been invited to a dinner one evening given by a foreign minister for Prince Li, who had been appointed viceroy to a southern province.

The Manchu's proud, egotistical countenance, devoid of feeling or sensitivity, reminded me of his humiliating setback on the Imperial Canal, and struck me all the more forcibly because his neighbor at the table—a pure Chinese—the powerful minister Yüan, had a refined face, alive with intellectual perception, delicate and humorous. The one clearly experienced nothing but his own desires and brutal caprices. The other, without ever losing awareness of his purpose in life, gave the impression of constantly seeking to maintain the grace of social relations. His whole fine, tolerant expression seemed to declare:

"No matter how bad things may get, let's be happy and content with one another."

A striking contrast between the two forces through which a goal can be reached: either brutal and senseless power, or benevolent and subtle intelligence.

Dinner over, I observed that Minister Yüan was momentarily alone, and I went to join him. He revealed at once an affectionate sympathy, motivated, he said, by the pleasure of meeting an occidental who spoke his language fluently. Then he questioned me concerning what I had seen and observed during my canal trip, adroitly drawing me out on points which interested him and finally bursting out with:

"But you must have met Prince Li?"

The tone of my answer no doubt betrayed strong emotion, for it seemed to capture both his attention and curiosity. The violent antipathy which the Prince's character aroused in me, the obscure certainty of finding an ally in my interlocutor, were strong enough to break down my prudent reserve: I related the whole adventure, including the discomfiture of the frustrated would-be kidnaper. The sharp-witted old man heard me out, his eyes gleaming. I was firmly convinced that he shared my feelings, but instead of the scathing comment I anticipated in respect to the tyrant's hired thugs, if not the tyrant himself, he merely asked me in a tone of keen interest:

"This Pei Yu . . . he must be endowed with a rare charm to attract so much attention. I congratulate you on having won his friendship; you will derive great pleasure from it. Did you say he sang with the Company of Increasing Virtue? Doubtless you have seen him again many times since your arrival in the capital?"

I had to admit that I had made no effort to see my little traveling companion again. He shook his head, his expression altered to one of censure and regret.

"You people from overseas are truly incomprehensible," he said. "You appreciate the delights of life as much as we do. And yet when the opportunity presents itself you remain impervious and indifferent, as if our life span—short and mainly filled with pain as it is—were endless and teeming with joys to be plucked at will. Ah, youth! You forget that a pleasure scorned may never be offered again."

Our conversation was soon interrupted. According to Chinese custom, the guests were taking their leave almost immediately after dinner.

Stung by the old gentleman's comments, and egged on by memories thus awakened, I betook myself the next day to the Theater of Increasing Virtue. I found none of the names I was looking for on the program. At the box office I was informed that Chang and his company had not yet returned. There had been no news of them.

Had Prince Li overtaken them then? Had they hidden out in

some large city in order to avoid their enemy? It was true, then, my pleasure had vanished for good!

7

Two weeks later I received an invitation from Minister Yüan for the following day. He was giving an intimate supper party. It was flattering to be invited by this charming old man who combined the contradictory gifts of a delicate and profound poet with those of genial financier and diplomat without peer in his field.

But the banquet tempted me little, despite the certainty that my palate would be tickled in various and unpredictable ways. What pleasure could one expect from a stag dinner?

Since none of the guests would be, for a certainty, my close friends, I could hardly expect the delights of intimacy from them. Pleasures of the mind, when the conversation is in a foreign tongue, quickly become an effort in concentration because of the difficulty of grasping a hundred veiled allusions to unknown persons and unfamiliar happenings. What satisfaction could I derive from these for either my career or my life?

Well, why deny it? Without friendship, without interest, social relationships quickly become burdensome when they are not lightened by the mystery of sexual attraction, just as the most delicious food is insipid if one neglects spices and salt. What strange notion brought about the exclusion of women from all festivities and social occasions in the Far East?

An orangey dusk was lacquering with delicate gold the last magenta of sunset as I clambered down from my mule-cart, stiff in every limb from the jolting and from having crouched down on the meager padding of the springless vehicle. I cursed the rule that forbade anyone in Peking except Princes of the Blood or Ministers of the Empire to ride in comfortable palanquins.

I arrived at a great door, its vermilion panels opened wide to a perspective of porticoes. A solemn butler, silk-robed, jewel-bonneted, awaited me, bowing at the threshold. He conducted me through the three palace courtyards sonorously announcing my name. In the third court, gnarled trunks of ancient cedars showed in black relief against the lights that illumined a pavilion off to one side. At the door my venerable host, standing amid the several guests who had already arrived, welcomed me with an amiable smile.

The sight of this sophisticate, second only to the Emperor in a nation with a population of five hundred million souls, thus stopping to receive a young barbarian—well-meaning, no doubt, but who to him must seem quite ignorant and boorish—brought to my mind painfully contrasting scenes: memories of the disdainful condescension shown to their guests by certain petty individuals inflated by the desire to impress with their advantages of wealth and position, unaware of any other stance in human relationships except insolence or obsequiousness.

The last guest had finally arrived and our host escorted us to our places. We all remained standing, waiting until he sat down before seating ourselves on the crimson cushions of our cloud-sculptured chairs, the mute invitations to celestial joys. He announced:

"To add to the pleasure of emptying our cups, I've asked some of our boy-actors to come brighten our supper. Of course each of us will have his favorite friend!"

As I marveled to myself how this chief of state could know who his friends' favorite little singers were, I intercepted his amused look in my direction. I was prey to a sudden suspicion. Was he offering his guests the spectacle of a foreigner's awkwardness when faced with the perfidious advances of one of those unscrupulous, unrestrained little scoundrels, the young actor-actresses called *hsiang-k'ung*, "the lordlings who assist"?

One by one the boys were already entering the room, wearing

bright-colored silken gowns, with long, shining, neatly plaited braids, the tops of their heads freshly shaven except for an elegant fringe, with painted faces and eyes alight with a knowing lasciviousness.

Followed by their guitarists, they came and sat down with an air of false modesty, each on an ottoman behind the one who sought his favors, exchanging the usual tender smiles and long handclasps.

A fresh and mellifluous voice, close by, suddenly jostled me from my musings.

"Has the Great Man been completely happy of late?"

Pei Yu was standing there, slender, elegant, graceful in his over-long embroidered robe, violet-colored like a glacier at sunset. He bowed and smiled, showing all his teeth pearly as rice grains, and awkwardly taking my hands in his as if to try to shake them in Western fashion. Our host's voice cut short my expressions of surprise:

"You aroused my curiosity by telling me about him. I sent out to find him, and now, thanks to you, we are good friends . . . Your description did not do him justice. But I could not forget your role in the favorable action of destiny, and I knew how happy you would both be to see one another again."

This little scene had drawn the attention of all those present at the table. I found myself extremely ill at ease under the rain of compliments and the knowing looks being thrown our way as the Minister related the saga of our voyage and the misadventure of Prince Li. Finally, my immediate neighbor leaned towards me and remarked enviously:

"I must congratulate you on your singular good fortune. You have at once acquired the friendship of our host, by giving him the delicate pleasure of knowing your friend, and the profound satisfaction of thwarting Prince Li, his undying adversary. The Prince is a long way off at this moment, but he receives complete reports from all over the Empire. He will certainly be sick with rage when he finds out you've made a fool of him."

As soon as the guests had finished their comments, I questioned Pei Yu. He told me how, after going ashore from our junk, the troupe had mingled with the crowd of spectators and had been able to get away from the canal and to cross town unobserved. They had walked until nightfall, then had asked hospitality at a farm set off the main road. In the subsequent days, once they were sure of not being followed, they traveled by easy stages until they reached the town of Tientsin. There they rented a house in the Foreign Concession, shielding themselves in this way from both the Chinese police and the machinations of the enemy. For a whole month they had worked without revealing their identity. Then they had risked a few performances. Finally the *shih fu* Chang had gone to Peking to prepare for their return. In Peking he was recognized by the Minister's agents, and they accompanied him back to Tientsin to fetch Pei Yu, whom Chang was only too happy to be able to guard from any surprise attack.

And so the lad, squeezing my hands in his long and supple fingers, expressed his gratitude to me:

"Thanks to you, I am now under the protection of the most powerful man in the Empire. I have nothing more to fear from the Prince. My fortune and my reputation are made. All the dangers and difficulties that beset me at the start are removed, thanks to you."

He was about to kneel for the great obeisance, the *k'o t'ou* and I was about to restrain him, when a joyful clamor arose.

"The distinguished gentleman from overseas has to forfeit a glass of liqueur and his friend must forfeit a song! They are the last ones to give one another an affectionate greeting."

We had to comply. I drained the tiny eggshell cup effortlessly and showed the company the empty bottom saying, as was the custom:

"K'an pei! My cup is dry!"

The lad, rising from where he sat beside me, asked:

"What tune would their lordships want to hear?"

"That is for our host, Custodian of the Wines, to decide," several voices cried out at once. "Let him speak!"

"Very well," the Minister responded, "Let us select some sweet and gay melody. The shepherdess' first song from *Hsiao Fang Niu:* 'At the third full moon, the peachtree bursts into blossom.'"

The pure tones of the boy's crystalline voice float rhythmically and harmoniously through the banquet chamber. The most melodious of birds fails to achieve the penetrating sweetness and piercing height of those notes unknown to occidental ears. Yet the diction remains clear and correct. What progress in so short a time!

Exclamations of surprise arise from the guests. Our host's changing expressions reveal a variety of complicated feelings: artistic enthusiasm, the joy of a connoisseur before a unique work of art . . . and surely, in his manner of looking at the boy . . . is that not love?

My sensitive spirit, attuned to the music that momentarily unifies the emotions of the listeners, becomes aware for the first time of the emotional lives of those who surrounded me. I am overwhelmed by the violence and strangeness of their passions; I feel myself far, far away from anything familiar—on the threshold of a world where pleasant sensations are no longer a crime, but the only reason for living, the sole aim of intelligence and reason.

Laughter had broken out again. Fines were inflicted lavishly. The hollow thrumming of guitars accompanied the penetrating tones of the shrill sopranos. The sweet savor and hot fumes of the "rose wine" tingled our palates and eyes. Viands of delicate but insistent flavor numbed our bodies with an agreeable lassitude. Live crayfish swam in brandy; bear paws and deer sinews followed a succulent soup of bird's nests and shark's fins. Fish and poultry had been prepared with minute care. Our taste buds, constantly stimulated by the succession of contrasting flavors, enjoyed without trying to identify the various delicacies, all finely chopped and served in rare porcelain bowls.

One of the guests recited a poem, every word of which seemed to me pregnant with meaning. My startled eyes beheld, without affront, one of my neighbors clasping "he-who-knows-his-heart," and with closed eyes, giving him wine drop by drop from lip to lip like a swallow feeding its young.

At this point one of the guests arose. I immediately recognized his austere face, which seemed as if illumined by inner life. He was one of the most influential in the literary academy, the Cedars-of-the-Forest-of-Brushes, the *Han Lin*, to which only the most eminent literary men were admitted. He had just been named Grand Marshal of the Armies of the Northern Ocean in an effort to infuse intellectual vigor among the officers whose brains had become atrophied by discipline and physical stress.

Raising his hand and obtaining a moment of attention, he said:

"O Master of the Wines! The grace and beauty of our young friends fills our hearts with rare joy. The music of their voices and their bird-like song transport our souls to the very portals of heaven, as far as paradise, the *T'ao-li-t'ien* where we share the happiness of Lao Tzu and his Immortals. Hasn't the moment come to restore our spirits with some *ling*, some verses of an unexpected turn? Shall we not compose quatrains whose meaning in each stanza will evoke the names of our friends? Shall we not try to renew the exploits of great poet Tu Fu and immortalize in one perfect poem the name and personality of each of our fellow guests?"

The question was evidently a serious one, for an anxious silence followed. Few of the guests attending felt equal to the genius of Tu Fu. The old man pondered a moment, then, turning toward me with a smile he enquired,

"In your beloved country have you no new and ingenious *ling* from your festivals that you would consent to teach us?"

Could I decently confess to the dismal, solemn boredom of our bourgeois dinner parties? Our insipid chatter, once depleted of private gossip, reduced to some public scandal or the latest play? Then, after dinner, the innocuous, racy anecdotes, ever the same, that have recently passed from the smoking room to the drawing room?

An idyll of the Greek poet Theocritus suddenly sang out from my memory . . . *Aïtés* "the tender friend." *Nisaioi megarees, aristenontes eretmois* . . .

> "O Megarians, sons of Nisus, master oarsmen,
>   May your happiness last for aye!
> Since you surpass all others who honor
>   Diocles of Attica, stranger and lover.
> Ever round his tomb at springtide you gather.
>   Youngsters to vie for the palm of kisses
> And he who presses lip on lip sweet beyond sweet
>   Goes home to mother crowned with laurels.

   Blest be the umpire of that kissing session!
     No doubt invokes he blue-eyed Ganymede and begs
   That his lips be his Lydian touchstone,
     To show the alchemist, base metal or pure gold."

I explained: "One of the ancient poets of our civilization had made famous a pastime which was renewed each year at his sepulcher for centuries. All the youth present chose a judge and he had to decide which of the youngsters gave the sweetest kiss."

There was a burst of enthusiasm. With a single sentence I had raised Europeans a hundredfold in the esteem of my fellow guests.

A brief discussion soon involved all the *hsiang-k'ung*. Our host, the Master of Wines, was naturally elected judge, and the serious examination began.

But after the third youth the old gentleman halted and announced gravely,

"I am much embarrassed. These first three contestants are each equally talented. It would do them a grave injustice to decide their merits lightly, after one superficial trial. I must petition my guests, one after the other, to take turns and savor those kisses that I am to receive. We then may discuss, with mutual understanding, the various merits of those "who-know our-hearts" while at the same time we may refer to ancient texts, poems or plays capable of shedding light on this ticklish subject."

Tactfully, then, he extended to all his guests the pleasure the Greeks had conceived for a single judge; to physical pleasure he added the dash and interest of an intellectual tourney.

It was indeed a brilliant joust, whose unlikely goal swiftly disarmed most of the dinner guests. They had all grown silent, attentive to the debate between the Cedar-of-the-Forest-of-Brushes and our host. Never, according to the comments of my immediate neighbors, had these two learned men performed with such joyous and original verve. What would I have given to have been able to record each quotation, every comment!

The supper was almost at an end. They were serving the fiftieth course when the judges declared their consciences sufficiently enlightened to vote for a winner of the contest. The dinner guests arose, conferred gravely with one another in little groups, then, separating, went into a huddle with other groups. The Cedar-of-the-Forest-of-Brushes passed from one to another, gathering votes. He came up to me, as if to ask my opinion, but whispered:

"Naturally, we're all voting for our host's friend, your favorite, Pei Yu. His comrades, understanding our idea, will not be jealous. I am sure that the Minister will be pleased."

We all resumed our seats. The last course, the traditional bowls of white rice, were placed on the table, a discreet way of telling the guests: My repast was so modest that you must still be hungry; refresh yourself ere we part.

Then the Cedar arose and addressed the Minister solemnly:

"O supreme judge! Your humble helpers, having exercised the faculties of their spirits in their desire to attain to the truth, have, like yourself, been forcibly struck by the equality of the talents subjected to their judgments. The lips of some have a nectar compared to which the sweetness of peach blossoms would seem coarse. The burning heat of certain others make the soul and intestines tremble. The piquant flavor of the other mouths is priceless. How to decide between such diverse, but equally troubling, virtues? One candidate alone seems to unite all gifts and to soar above his fellow contestants, even as you yourself soar above us all. It is Pei Yu. And our unanimous vote proclaims him winner of this contest in the European manner."

Our host inclined his head:

"Despite my many years of constant study, I am, alas! convinced of my inexperience concerning the savor of kisses, for it always seems to me that the lips of my most recent love have the most intoxicating flavor. This evening, humble man of letters that I am, I am still dizzy from the learned quotations and admirable poems that you revealed to me on this burning issue. Deeply thankful for your help, I dare not challenge your judgment. Pei Yu is therefore declared the fairest lily among the fairest lilies. As reward, I shall ask him a favor, and adopt him as my *kan-êrh-tzu*, my dry son."

A storm of applause followed.

These foster parenthoods are a charming custom of the Flowery

Empire. When friends are sure enough of one another, they declare themselves "dry brothers," enjoying thenceforth the mutual privileges of brotherhood and of being treated as such by other family members.

Depending on differences in age and differing degrees of sentiments, one chooses either a foster uncle, a foster sister or a foster father, who then greets one using the adoptive title, adding in this way an appearance of kinship to a strong bond of affection. Pei Yu, on hearing this flattering decision, ran forward to kneel before the master of the house, repeating,

"How dare I accept such a favor? I am unworthy of such kindness."

But as the Minister, smiling, remained seated with his open hands outstretched, the youth understood that no further delay was in order. He lowered his forehead thrice to the carpet, each time arising and starting the obeisance over again until he had accomplished the "three times three" prostrations required by ritual. Then, still kneeling, he placed his hands within the Minister's, and pronounced the sacred formula. "You are my father's equal, and I shall behave as your own son forever."

The Minister concluded the "dry" adoption with simple words: "O my son!"

Drawing the boy gently up, he then took from his own wrist a finely chased bracelet of gold and placed the antique masterpiece on the boy's wrist. This solemn gesture, accomplished in the presence of witnesses, was as binding as the most formal written document.

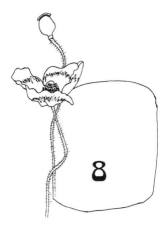

8

The table companions, now reunited and standing, gave the lad an ovation. I also noticed from among the rest of the *hsiang-k'ung* who had joined the throng such envious looks that I felt my blood freeze.

But the elderly Minister approached me and, taking me by the hand, led me towards a large *k'ang*, a divan closed on three sides by a lacy scuptured fretwork where graceful foliage twined and blossomed in a disordered fantasy of forms and colors.

He made me lie facing him on the other side of a tray on which glowed a little covered lamp, and the "hundred treasures of the smoker"—everything one needed to smoke opium. Pei Yu, soon released, had come to join us, and sat huddled against him, dipping a long needle into an opium of exquisite fragrance, which I quickly identified as being one of the purest products of the Upper Yunnan.

As he supervised the boy's activity, watching while Pei Yu twirled the swelling bead of opium in the heat of the lamp, the old gentleman said to me:

"Truly, there is no greater happiness on earth than loving. We arrive in the world and our first joy is to feel the sweet warmth of our mother's breast. There we find a voluptuous engulfment, a deep feeling of security that dissipates all our anxieties and assuages our bitterest tears. And it is perhaps the unconscious memory of this first utter happiness that attracts us for a long time to the love of women."

The lad handed him the heavy pipe of carved ivory. He inhaled the pale blue smoke deeply without pausing, at last permitting it slowly to escape from his lungs. I murmured:

"Twenty-five centuries ago the philosopher Mi-Tzu had already seen the truth. Love dictates all actions. Beauty, grace, tenderness attract us unceasingly. But Yang-Ti, who flourished about the same time, maintained that hate and the desire to do harm are the real motives of all our actions, was he not also correct in a sense? And if Yang-Ti is right, is not Mi-Tzu wrong?"

"We often discuss this problem," he replied. "To my way of thinking Mi-Tzu and Yang-Ti each based their systems on observations that were correct, but incomplete. Hence neither arrived at the heart of the question. The egotistical and cold-blooded cat loves to torture the mouse it is about to kill. The warm-hearted, devoted dog prefers his master's blows to indifference. In the same manner, poets and artists are emotionally overwhelmed by the experience of Beauty, of Goodness. Evil-doers are delighted only by upsetting everyone they encounter and causing them suffering and endless annoyance. But what actually are both seeking if not the satisfaction of their unconscious desires? The former love only smiles, sweetness, tender words. The latter love only tears, anger and discontent while Beauty, Wit and Sensibility mean nothing to them.

"They all delight, however, in the satisfaction they experience from realizing their blind impulses. We should only give heed to satisfying our heart's desire: the object and the means count for little. It is for each one of us to seek out the beings or things that help us to obtain this satisfaction. Above all, it is for each one of us to recognize, to fend off or to flee all that may hinder the daily attainment of our satisfaction."

"Is there no risk here of being led on to our ruin, my Lord?" I objected.

"It is enough that we let ourselves be guided by Reason and that we never attract a major evil through tasting a minor delight. But destiny makes us what we are, and dictates the circumstances of our lives. Can we know, in any case, what constitutes our ruin? Is it not brought on by the most heroic actions as well as by the greatest crimes? Death is the same for all, and the soldier who defends his country may be annihilated no less than the gallows bird. And what is there after death? No one knows."

He drew slowly on a second pipe. Then, caressing Pei Yu's pearly cheeks with his long, slender fingers, he continued:

"As for me, I love the sweetness and brilliance of rose petals, and what rose could rival this cheek? I love the profound vivaciousness of eyes glowing softly with the luster of pearls, when those glances are the expression of a lofty mind, a soul of moonlike purity, full of the language of flowers. I love the supple warmth of the human body, softer than that of a cat or bird. I love the jadelike purity of children's voices. I love youth's subtle innocence, the candid violence of its desires, its lack of prejudice, its enthusiasm for new ideas and things. Who better than these charming children can give me all this?"

"But many women are just what you have described, my Lord."

He shook his head.

"When you too have attained a declining maturity, you will have known all the different types of women: their well-worn tricks that deceive only those whose eyes are closed to Reason; their absurd and stubborn caprices inspired by their physical instability; their bad faith; their constant infidelities, great or small; their fanatical devotion to fashion and current fads; their complete dismay at being without children, their total frenzy over those they do have . . ."

"But, my Lord," I interrupted, "there are companions who have beautiful and lofty souls, noble, unchanging, perfect First Wives, the ones in whom we find once again the sure sweetness of the maternal breast, a friend's faithful indulgence coupled with the intoxicating passion of a lover."

"Alas!" he sighed, "they are rare indeed, those Precious Ones among the Precious Ones. Yet, if by great good fortune such a one comes our way, her lofty qualities themselves isolate us from her by confining her to the noble function of mistress of hearth and home, guardian of the traditions of our race. We are forced to pursue our intellectual lives independent from her. She does not share our constant mental development. We cannot relegate *her* to the role of supper-entertainer. Alas, how under these conditions can woman be a man's real companion in his studies and his pleasures?"

"But what of love, my Lord?"

"Love is vile and bestial when it depends only on the act and is not born of mutual attraction, of an unfailing comprehension of the unspoken. Now, in what beings could we find more intellectual and moral understanding, and more seduction, than in these youths? They give their entire day to memorizing the rarest classics. They are thoroughly shaped by the noblest thoughts, the most delicate poems and the finest flashes of wit. They dream only of distinguishing themselves before our eyes, of capturing our esteem. Pei Yu already gives me as much pleasure through conversation as I derive from listening to his pure voice, from contemplating his freshness."

"But, my Lord, could not young girls arouse equally strong feelings?"

"Young girls are female. They are susceptible to the fleeting moment, never to immutable Reason. And furthermore, being female their first thoughts are for their eventual progeny, they all dream of being taken to the bridal chamber. But these youths are not concerned with wedlock, being unable to provide us with descendants, they do not arouse the jealousy of our First Wives. Moreover, trust my vast experience . . ."

Here he leaned forward, his expression serious. ". . . Believe me, the love of women is in every way like peaches overripened by the sun. Their sweetness, their vivid hues, their velvet smoothness tempt us and render us drunk with desire. But once we've bitten down, they immediately lose their crispness and melt, leaving in the mouth nothing but a warm, sweetish liquid."

"And the love of men?" I inquired.

"Ah! The love of men!" He cried out almost lyrically, " I should compare it to an apple, plain in appearance, without down, without mystery. But its crunchy and slightly dry freshness stimulates the palate even while satisfying it. It does not melt away mushily, but grows firmer and firmer until it is no more."

9

Next day I was awakened by urgent knocking at my door. I grumbled, "Come in," and my manservant entered. Despite the muddled condition of my awakening mind, I observed his dignified and offended air as he stood on the threshold and announced:

"The *shih fu* Chang insists on speaking with the Great One. He allegedly has serious news to impart. To me, however, he seems to be rather unbalanced. The Great One should be on guard and not let his heart cloud his mind."

The respectable majordomo had never approved of my relations with the young singers and their teacher. On board the junk his attitude had occasionally annoyed me. Now I was strongly tempted to seize the opportunity to poke fun at his former disapproval. But to chide an oriental at the wrong time makes him shut up like a clam, and one loses his confidence forever. So I composed my features and replied:

"If that's the way things are, bring him up. But stay behind him and be ready to grab him at the first sign of trouble."

And to myself I added: That way your curiosity will be satisfied. You will not imagine a mysterious relationship between this individual and your master. Your confidential mission will swell your own self-esteem and will give you added "face" in the household. You will redouble your efforts to serve me.

Chang was already there, his face all haggard and bloodstained.

His appearance was appalling indeed. He flung himself on his knees before me, crying out:

"Save us, Great One, save us!"

Still on his knees, despite my words of welcome, he continued, sobbing: "Pei Yu . . . Pei Yu . . . "

"Well?"

"Vanished. Kidnaped."

"Kidnaped? Where? How did it happen? I left him a few hours ago."

In his distress he could barely reply. I made him sit down and administered cognac. He finally pulled himself together and described what had happened.

When the Minister's banquet had ended late that night, Chang had carefully stowed Pei Yu away in the narrow confines of his mule-cart. He himself, ever armed with his heavy revolver, took his seat according to custom on one of the shafts, while the groom trotted on the other side.

The trip to the house recently given them by their new protector was not a long one. The establishment was located in a secluded quarter where a felon would have waited in vain for a victim, so out-of-the-way that there was not even a police patrol.

At that hour of the night in Peking, the profound silence is broken only by the sounds of gongs serving to alert and frighten off prowlers and proving to the citizens that their watchmen are awake. Each hour the brazen voices of bells resound from the clock tower and reverberate above the one-storied houses. And every second hour the nightwatch is punctuated by the deep resonance of the giant gong in its square tower. The transparent air, pervaded by starlight, is so pure, so clear that even beyond the walls of the Inner City one may often hear cries, calls and laughter, and even brawls breaking out in suburban gambling dens.

In this nocturnal peace, to the rhythm of the mule's hooves, to the rumbling of wheels, the sleepy *shih fu* and his charge had almost arrived at their destination and were turning in to the narrow lane where they lived, when a band of men fell upon them.

In spite of his surprise, Chang had been able to draw his revolver, killing one aggressor and wounding another. But the blow of a heavy cudgel had felled him unconscious in the dusty road.

When he came to, a gray and violet dawn already touched the eroded walls of the alley. There was not a trace of the carriage, the groom, the dead body or the rest of the assailants. At first he thought he had been dreaming, but when he moved, the pain in his head and the clotted blood on his clothes were evidence of the horrifying truth: Pei Yu had been kidnaped.

He rushed to their house nearby. The boy was not there nor was the mule-cart.

Chang still had the energy to run to the palace of the Minister, who happened to be leaving at that precise moment for the dawn audience. He heard the whole story from his palanquin. Summoning one of his secretaries he gave him some brief instructions and left. Dismissed without being reassured, the *shih fu* had then come directly to me.

My first question was whether he had recognized his assailants.

"None of them. I had no clue. At first I thought of Prince Li. But he left the capital ten days ago."

"Has anyone else shown a particular interest in Pei Yu?"

"No. Who would have the nerve to offend the all-powerful Minister Yüan?"

Certainly only Prince Li would have dared. But he was gone. The Emperor perhaps? . . . Though he could scarcely be concerned in such a matter. The problem seemed insoluble. But to reassure the *shih fu* I said to him,

"Calm down. The boy will soon be back. The Lord Yüan's will is the law of the Empire."

But Chang shook his head.

"Whoever dared kidnap Pei Yu must be quite sure of immunity, even if he is discovered. And me—who is to say that I won't be charged with murder?"

"I don't believe it," I objected. "In order to do that your attackers would have to make themselves known. They would certainly prefer to remain incognito. Still and all, anyone in your shoes should think seriously of taking a little trip, to avoid assassination."

"Leave town? Abandon Pei Yu?" he murmured plaintively.

"Do you feel you are more powerful than the Minister? In any case if you need, help please know that you can call on me."

No doubt he expected such a promise, for he seemed relieved and answered:

"I am deeply grateful to you for extending your celestial protection to me. You are right. I'll take the morning train for Tientsin. If you have any news, I beg you to get in touch with me. I'll give my address to the Chief of Foreign Affairs in Tientsin."

After making a deep reverence, he hurried away.

My majordomo was swollen with self-importance, being involved in a drama in which highly placed personages were actors. He could not resist giving me some advice.

"This Chang," he said, "is not really evil, but his reputation is terrible. Your Lordship asked me nothing about it when we were traveling. So I said nothing. Now I dare to speak. He is not a *cheng-tsung-jên*, a correct and honorable man."

"What crime has he committed?"

"Then your Lordship has not suspected? The little slaves that Chang buys are not all equally talented in music, singing, recitation and dancing. Does my Lord know what happens to the children who fail in theater?"

"I don't. He re-sells them, I suppose."

"Most company directors do. Chang has another way. He has opened low-price restaurants where these lads function apparently as *hsiang-k'ung* for poor people."

"That doesn't appear too reprehensible to me."

"But the fact is," he replied, leaning toward me confidentially, "these restaurants are not really restaurants at all. They all have a little door in the back leading to another house. And that is where the drunken customers drag the little boys who earlier were egging them on to drink. And despite the modest prices, these houses bring in, it is said, much more than his theater does. It's hardly respectable to run such a business, do you not agree?"

"You are right. He is dominated by avarice and far-removed from the accepted ideal of a gentleman. However, he doesn't matter.

We must give our full support to Lord Yüan. So be careful! Don't talk. Keep your ears open. Wild horses can never drag back all the words that jump the fence of our teeth."

10

The unconcealed approval extended to me by the First Minister of the Empire inevitably brought down upon my head the oily and self-interested attentions of sycophants, those "summer patriots" who gravitate toward whomever has been touched by the unpredictable favors of destiny, in the vain hope that they too will benefit from the divine rays and profit by their wealth-producing reflections.

Hardly was the morning over before I received a large red envelope with an invitation covered by ideograms which were cunningly arranged on the page. In the top right corner of the envelope, written in tiny letters to suggest the humility of the author, the words "Respectfully sent." Then, in huge characters, doubly respectful: "To the Great Man." Below to the left, in medium characters: " . . . may he deign to open it."

The letter itself, written on auspicious scarlet paper, bore the customary formula.

"He who respectfully sends this awaits humbly until . . . the Shining One descends to his side. He has prepared goblets and cakes for the Hour of the Chickens, and . . . " (the rest in humble characters) " . . . awaits, crouched in reverence, head held low."

The Hour of the Chickens, beginning at five o'clock and ending at seven, indicated that it would be a theater party. Invitations are usually timed for the Hour of the Dog, from seven to nine in the evening.

The large visiting card, also on red paper, that accompanied the invitation was that of a fellow guest of the previous evening, a person named Wang.

It has been said that it is easy to tell a man's character by the look of his visiting card. According to this criterion, Wang was ambitious, for the format of his card was exaggerated; vain, because the ideograph representing his name was unusually large; not brutal, but not energetic, for the brush strokes were thin.

Wang, as it turned out, was one of those persons of whom it is difficult to say whether they inspire more laughter or disgust. He had achieved his civil post not through his intellectual merit, but by clever employment of his fortune and family influence. Those around him took a lively interest in the devious bargaining he pursued in order to obtain a post of provincial governor that would match his grade, and at the cheapest price.

Capricious Nature had not endowed him with beauty along with fortune. Thin and gawky, it was said that his body temperature was too high, for his cadaverous face was always decorated with a crop of red pimples. His long, bulbous nose was covered by so many of them that it shone like a beacon. Because of this trait, his friends all came to know him as "The Amorous Ass."

The fact that he had bought his job in no way diminished his literary pretensions. His conversation was studded with classical quotations, often misused, so that his listeners would shake with irrepressible hilarity. He would then be astounded by his own wit. His eyes, rimmed in scarlet by a chronic case of inflammation would grow large as scaly saucers. His lips, already too short, would draw back to reveal whitish gums above long, yellowed teeth. In such moments he had the impressive appearance of one of those decapitated heads that are hung by their pigtails like bunches of grapes at the massive gates of towns and villages during times of crisis.

When my host greeted me at the threshold of his reception hall, the setting sun was still giving off fierce rays. The golden light only accentuated the worn poverty of a commonplace decor: heavy, unyielding chairs lacquered with vermilion and outlined in black; rectangular tables, also in vermilion lacquer. On the walls hung some white paper scrolls bearing a few classical precepts inscribed with wide brush strokes by well-known people.

All appearances led one to believe that here must be the most modest establishment in the city. To seem poor serves its purpose. All over the world wealth has a keen interest in concealing itself behind a façade of poverty in order to escape excessive taxation.

In the meantime my host continued his distasteful bowing and scraping. Having satisfied himself that all his guests knew one another, he invited us to sit down at the table. There were not many of us, only eight.

Our host, watchful of modest appearances, had provided only one *hsiang-k'ung*. Because on such occasions one looks for gaiety more than love-making, a *ch'ou* is invited, rather than an ingenue.

I recognized Precious Treasure, the ungainly little boy who had acted with such imagination on our river journey. He was the master of ceremonies and according to custom was given the place of honor before the bowl of ham cut in thin slices.

After an exchange of polite greetings, the first dishes were served. Despite Wang's efforts, conversation languished. Our host then asked Precious Treasure:

"What *ling* are you going to propose today to enliven our toasts?"
And the lad, already full of confidence, replied:

"The best game among intellectuals is the one called *ta-lei t'ai* or 'boxing match.' Each player in turn proposes a verse to his neighbor, who must immediately find another verse of corresponding sense. Whoever loses must naturally do as bidden by the winner. But we shall regulate these penalties in advance. The first loser must drink three cups."

"And the second?" cried the table companions, now full of interest.

"The second shall drink five. The third loser must . . . must imitate a *hsiang-k'ung* offering a cup to his friend."

Everyone laughed. Again it was asked:

"What will the fourth one do?"

"He will also imitate a *hsiang-k'ung* and his friend, but in a different manner. Today, to make the game harder, we shall select poems from the T'ang Dynasty only."

When I tried to excuse myself by reason of incompetence, a rather stiff penalty was immediately imposed. I was happy to be able to bring it off as well as I did. Then the game began according to the established rules. The two first losers downed their numerous libations with much grimacing.

The "Amorous Ass" was the third loser. Rising with alacrity he seized a cup with both hands. His entire body trembled with his efforts to make himself graceful. He wriggled his hips and, simpering, tortured his lipless mouth into a seductive leer so hideous that it horrified me, but had the other guests rocking with laughter. Their mirth redoubled when, proud of his success, he leaned toward his neighbor and spoke in honey-sweet tones:

"Will the Lord of my heart permit me to present him respectfully with this glass and will he deign to give me 'face' by accepting it?"

All the while he was amorously rolling his red-rimmed eyes in a manner that was utterly atrocious.

Laughter subsided at last and the game continued. All were impatient to see how the next loser would contrive to ape the airs of a *hsiang-k'ung*. The lot fell to a strapping young fellow with a simple, good-humored expression. Would he be able to portray a graceful and refined boy-actor?

Calmly he plucked a large golden chrysanthemum from a vase and stuck it in his hair. Then, bearing the full beaker in both his hands, he tripped with mincing steps toward his winner and bowed, saying:

"O my Lord, long has your amorous ardor pursued me in vain with its fire. Touched by your constancy, today I wish to grant you a favor, and present you with *tseng-p'i p'ei*, a 'cup of flesh.'"

The other watched him uncertain and amused. The loser had already filled his mouth with a great draught of liquor. Quickly lowering his face to the other's as for a tender kiss, he disgorged the wine into the mouth of the unlucky winner, who was so taken aback that he coughed, sneezed and cried out to such an extent that he spat out all the wine, drenching the face and robe of the loser, who was shaking with laughter.

The entire company was overjoyed. For once the classical quotations of our host met with unreserved success when he declaimed sententiously:

"The sage has said, 'One must learn just how to offer wine to one's friends.'"

Then he added:

"This reminds me that, recently, two of my wives while trying to console one another during my absence got into the same bed together. When they had undressed, just for a joke one lay on top of the other and pretended to replace me, imitating the motions imposed on us by Nature. In their innocent ardor they soon discovered an extreme pleasure in this game . . . a tangible pleasure. When they had calmed down a little after these agreeable transports, one of them said, 'In order not to forget this diversion, we must give it a name. Suppose we call it 'polishing the mirror'?

"The other thought a moment, then suddenly broke out laughing: 'I have found a better one. Given the abundance of our amorous dew, and our position, we ought to call it *tseng-p'i p'ei*, offering a "cup of flesh."'"

The anecdote had the success it deserved. It excited the jealousy of one guest, who exclaimed:

"You may very well go on about polishing the mirror. But do you know which are the three best-polished things in the world?"

Since no one replied, he counted them out on his fingers: "The heads of the Buddhist priests, polished by razors; women's thighs, by constant friction; and the lips of the *hsiang-k'ung*, from kisses."

And then rushing up to Precious Treasure he wanted to receive proof of the truth of the proverb. In the hilarious confusion that ensued, most of the guests got to their feet giddy with laughter and drink.

Since the beginning of the meal, Precious Treasure had been sending me glances whose meaning I could not fathom. I took advantage of the hubbub to approach him and ask him what he wanted of me. Confused, he replied:

"Me? Nothing—"

He was cut short. Our host cried out jokingly.

"I caught you. You were whispering illicit propositions to the foreign gentleman. You are wasting your time. Pei Yu has already captured his heart."

But at this name, a sour smile twisted the youth's features.

"Pei Yu? It will be some time before we see him again."

"On the contrary, his new 'dry father' will allow him to continue his stage career. Otherwise it would be a case of beauty buried. He said as much."

Precious Treasure chuckled on without answering. So he knew all about the kidnaping of his former victim and was gloating over it. How could he be so well informed? Through Chang? I wanted to find out, and I asked him:

"What has become of your *shih fu*? Have you seen him of late?"

"Heavens, no! He has had himself replaced at the theater so that he can spend all of his time with his precious Pei Yu." Since he had spoken neither to Chang, nor certainly to my servant, he must have been informed through other channels. I was struck by an idea—did he know the abductors?

Leaving the lad to his courtiers, I went to thank Wang for his invitation, pretending that I believed it would be the only one. Then I congratulated him on his amusing friend. He immediately protested:

"I am not his patron. I haven't the means."

Pretending indifference, I asked casually:

"Has he a protector already?"

"What? Didn't you know?" answered Wang, delighted to be able to show off his knowledge of theater life. "The Beileh Fan, Prince Li's cousin, never fails to invite him to his banquets, and claims he is the only *ch'ou* who can really make him laugh. In any case you shall witness his triumph. We are going to hear him this evening."

He looked at his two watches and motioned his servants to bring cups of tea, mute signals of impending departure.

I saw him slip a silver ingot weighing over ten ounces into Precious Treasure's sleeve. Then amid gales of laughter we left the hall and got into our carriages, which looked like little boxes on wheels.

11

On entering the huge amphitheater, I was at first confused by the lights, noise, laughter and chatter, and by the sharp fumes of the crude tobacco of Peking. One could hardly distinguish the shrill voices of the singers through the intermittent thunder of gongs and cymbals, the penetrating whine of fiddles, and the cicada-like strumming of guitars.

Our seats were in the balcony, a wide gallery occupying three sides of the rectangular hall and supported by a row of heavy columns, formerly painted vermilion. A box had been reserved for us, just above the square platform that served as a stage and to the right, over the violins, and far away from the gongs.

Once again while observing the audience, I was struck by the total absence of women among the spectators. Elegant silken robes, well-plaited tresses and beardless faces here and there made up for this complete lack of a feminine element that would have been shocking to a European audience.

In the box next to ours there sat in state an individual whose brutal face looked familiar to me under his sable bonnet. He wore a white-tipped gray astrakhan vest worth its weight in gold.

Numerous servants were busily engaged in serving him. One passed him a water-pipe of chased silver. Another poured an amber-colored tea into a covered cup, holding carefully in its caddy a rare porcelain teapot that would remain hot for hours. Others were setting out a number of plates of pastries on a table.

Two *hsiang-k'ung* with painted faces were standing next to the man in the astrakhan vest, stroking his shoulders and seemingly pleading with him. But his expression remained sour and his grumbling voice could be heard above the tumult.

"You especially, Pei-lin. I spent over five thousand cash on you. Yet I haven't seen you for a week."

The boy's shrill voice pleaded with him. I could only distinguish a sentence now and then.

"The First Wife is kind. But the Fifth, I Tai Tai, beat me the last time she saw me leave your bedchamber. She said that after me you were unappetizing."

The memory of that scene must have been agreeable, for it brought a smile to the man's hard features.

"Never fear. She won't touch you again."

"I don't want to be beaten," insisted the boy.

"Very well, I shall give you a pavilion, just like my wives. But be very careful not to receive any visitors there. Or else I'll have you beaten to death."

On stage, warriors jousted, their faces painted with violent colors. These were the *Wu-shêng.* Their shoulders bristled with tiny flags and were weighed down by armor flashing with countless metal disks and plaques. They brandished weapons of our Middle Ages— heavy maces, battle axes, flails with steel balls, long spears—and they engaged in complicated and skillful fencing, changing formation according to the ancient drill of warlike ballets, their every step punctuated by the clangor of gongs and cymbals. *K'ang-chieh, Tai-chieh* was the name given this ancient rhythm by the musicians. Furthermore, at artfully chosen intervals the air was rent by the blaring of long copper trumpets.

Sometimes two men, their torsos bare, their heads tightly wrapped in turbans, attacked one another with swords upraised. But just when the broad, heavy blades would seem about to split them asunder, they would dodge the blow by rolling on their backs, to spring up instantly and face their opponent. Occasionally one of them, more agile than the other, would uncoil like a spring and leap clear over his adversary's head.

Then the procession of heavily armored *wu-shêng* was formed again leading the way at last for the victorious emperor, surrounded by all the bearded actors, the *hu-tzu*. These performers had faces decorated with monumental beards down to their belts and either stroked them majestically or blew them out furiously, spitting like angry cats. Here were the last vestiges of vanished costumes and customs hardly mentioned in history.

To the left of our box, on the balcony, were set the buffet tables. A respectable burgher, peacefully smoking his bubbling waterpipe, was already installed at one of them.

Two young men, plainly clad, sat down next to him. From their timid glances and awkward postures, I guessed them to be new arrivals in the capital—natives of Shansi province, to judge by their fair complexions.

I was not the only one to recognize them as provincials, for the attendant who came to collect the entrance fee charged them double the regular price. A few minutes later it was the tea and pastry vendor who cheated them shamelessly.

Then an old women, carrying a tray basket full of small objects, approached them. She held up for their inspection a small jade pipe mounted with silver. She whined:

"*Lao-yeh!* Your Lordships! Here's a bargain for you! A beautiful pipe. I'm selling it today for nothing."

It was, in fact, a very pretty trinket. One of the young men took it, examined it and inquired the price. The crone replied sharply:

"I paid twenty-five ounces of silver for it. It is an antique and anyone can tell you that you won't find one like it in all the capital for less than thirty *liang*." The young man, unconvinced, shook his head and tried to give her back the pipe. The woman would not take it, saying:

"I paid twenty-five *liang* for it, and I can't afford to cut the price even a copper *ch'ien*. However, in your case, and because we have never done business before, I shall ask only fifteen *liang*."

The young man shook his head again. The old lady took back the pipe reluctantly and asked with an offended air:

"Well, how much do you offer?"

The young man, hoping to be rid of her, replied:

"I'll give two ounces, not a penny more."

"Two ounces! You must be joking. Nothing less than six."

She turned away with dignity and walked a few paces. But hearing no one call her back, she returned and held out the pipe, grumbling:

"Very well. Take it for two *liang*, since you don't mind ruining a poor old woman."

The young man became embarrassed, blushed, looked to his companion as if for help, then stammered:

"I . . . er . . . I don't have that much with me. I prefer to buy it from you tomorrow."

"That doesn't matter," said the old woman. "I'll go to your house with you."

"We . . . we live a long way from here."

"That doesn't matter."

At a loss for an answer, he agreed. As he held out his hand a stir of spectators leaving their seats jostled the old woman. She lost her balance and dropped the pipe. It shattered into several fragments.

Slowly and without recriminations, she picked up the pieces of jade. Then she placed them on the table before the young man and announced firmly:

"You could have had the whole pipe for two ounces. But the pieces are worth six *liang*."

The provincials protested violently. The old woman then raised her voice and in a sharp tone cried out against the injustice that she was being forced to undergo. All of the spectators turned toward the balcony.

The young men, terrified by the scandal, were already caving in. They glanced at each other questioningly and were about to yield, ready to make any concession to save face. But the worthy burgher sitting next to them gave the table a resounding smack with the flat of his hand and cried out in indignation.

"That pipe is hardly worth a *liang*. This is robbery. If these two give you a half a string of cash for it, you'll be well paid. They are not responsible for your loss. If you don't accept, I shall call the police."

At the dreaded word "police," several nearby spectators arose and disappeared hastily in the direction of the exit. Prudence is the mother of safety. The old woman, suddenly pacified, exclaimed:

"Good! Good!"

And she hastened to make off, without even checking the number of coppers strung on cord that the provincial had drawn from his sleeve and handed to her.

Meanwhile on stage, the martial maneuvers had given way to comic skits from daily life. Precious Treasure, his nose daubed with white as befitted a clown, had captured the attention of the house and was getting laughs for his irresistible pantomime as much as for his lines.

He played the part of an old man chosen to arbitrate in a family quarrel between a woman and her sister-in-law. His anxiety to avoid becoming involved in the argument, his efforts to calm the participants without agreeing with either of them, his comical anguish before the fury of the embattled women—all were played with that art of under-statement, a feeling for the essential that seemed more real than life itself.

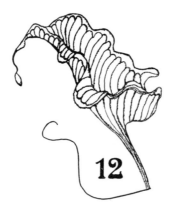

12

When the show was over the "Amorous Ass" dragged me off
into the wings. I was greatly astonished, since I had always been told
that it was neither fitting nor proper to risk being seen in the backstage
area. A man in an official position does not visit the *hsiang-k'ung;* he
sends for them. One has no guarantee that he will not be subjected to
some humiliating joke at the hands of thirty to forty adolescents drunk
with success and knowing full well that their victims would never
brave the ridicule of a lawsuit. Wang was quite aware of all this, but
lust inspires us to risk the gravest dangers.

He led me toward the exit and along the alley outside the building, until we reached a small stage door in the rear, which he pushed
open to reveal the greenroom. The huge chamber was a kaleidoscope
of movement and color, as confusing as a cage full of parrots. Actors,
supers, musicians and visitors were all there milling about, dressing,
undressing, putting on make-up, singing at the top of their voices, re-
hearsing or exchanging jokes, in an extraordinary jumble of seething
life and youthful gaiety.

A young boy, completely naked, was squatting on the floor in a
corner peering into a mirror in his make-up box. Evidently he was
afraid to soil his sumptuous costumes while making up. He already
sported a wig and was carefully shaving his eyebrows in order to paint
them on again a little higher, "à la butterfly," with a fine, clean line that
would accentuate his virginal, innocent features.

Wang stopped and said a few words to him. Wang's eyes glittered lewdly as they lingered on that soft, rounded creamy flesh devoid of pubic hair, and the boy smiled as if excited by this scrutiny.

As we continued our way, Wang murmured to me, "That's the famous Tsin-lin, who has completely ruined all his lovers. One was reduced to suicide; another to such poverty that he was forced to sell his wives and children. Another, mad with jealousy, tried to kill him. Fortunately the knife slashed only his robe. It would have been a great pity to destroy such maddening flesh, for it is enough to reduce one's bones to jelly at the sight."

A swordsman, attired in the *wu-shêng* style in a short, tight vest that left his chest bare, had cleared the space around him as he exercised his wrists by twirling two large sabers until they resembled steel lightning.

A young actor, pompous and solemn in his emperor's robes, paraded up and down uttering noble pronouncements.

Loud outcries were heard repeatedly. A door in the backdrop would close on a vanishing warrior in a nightmare mask. We could still hear his heavy steps punctuated by gongs. To our left, from another exit door, sprang panting swordsmen or soldiers dragging decapitated dummies.

Here and there squatted groups of extras dressed in humble costumes as porters, beggars or palanquin bearers. Smoking their short, tiny-bowled metal pipes, they gloomily watched the fans pressing wantonly around the young actors who were making up.

Most of these old workhorses had in their youth also known the joys of being courted, of applause. But the fatal passing of puberty had robbed them of the piercing vocal quality demanded by the public. Their figures, once pliant, had hardened, then changed shape. The exacting devotees, who tire just as rapidly of muscular male hardness as of sweet feminine plenitude, had turned away from them at the same moment that grace, youth and tender beauty were abandoning them as well.

Leaving the "Amorous Ass" to the joys of being caressed by four or five of his little friends, I stopped to observe Precious Treasure who, having removed his white wig and his long greybeard's robe, was scrubbing from his face the disfiguring clown white and blue wrinkles.

He continued his operation in silence for a while, then he gave me a quick sideways glance and said, with an expression of insincere regret:

"I'm afraid they'll never discover the kidnaper of Pei Yu."

So he knew that the kidnaping had taken place. I questioned him sharply:

"Who told you that he had been kidnaped?"

For a moment he looked confused, but quickly regained his composure.

"Who? . . . Everybody. The whole town is talking about the fury of his friend, the Minister."

And he chuckled maliciously. There could be no doubt. The kidnaper was certainly the Beileh Fan, Precious Treasure's protector. And Fan was undoubtedly working for Prince Li.

At this moment someone was approaching us. Precious Treasure continued calmly:

"So you think that in this role I should stoop over more and bleat more like a goat? I'll try it next time. You must come and see me again."

Standing by the door, I took a last look around. Dirty plaster had fallen from crumbling walls, revealing gray, ill-laid bricks from which hung dusty spider webs. There was no ceiling; the undersides of tiles could be seen and the rafters were black with soot.

Yet in that wretched barn, color, music, wealth, love, battle, all the illusions of existence were produced by a few worn-out slaves and by children so disturbing in their androgynous grace that an entire population contemplating them could forget the sovereign attraction of women.

Outside in the alley filled with fresh air and starlight, Wang hindered my every step. Still completely intoxicated by these transvestite beauties, he declaimed a hundred poems; he called on me to witness his literary and artistic sensibility. His enthusiasm broke all bounds in historical quotations, in grandiose clichés of admiration for the ancient generals whose modern evocation we had witnessed. But all his literary effervescence failed to disguise the boiling-over of his lust for the slender, panting youths who were exiting the stage, their skins alive and warm from their recent efforts.

I thought then of those pious souls who at this very moment were attending High Mass on the other side of the world, in my good little native French town. What indignant horror they would have felt if they could have seen all this!

What would the priest in white alb have thought or said? At this moment he might be preaching the irreconcilable contradiction of a God of goodness who had created hell and the devil in order to eternally punish souls that He Himself had drawn from the void, omnisciently understanding that they could never resist the temptations He had so carefully prepared. God punished these very bodies, His own creations, with all kinds of erotic desires, finally holding up to them the example of the Virgin Mary, who became a mother although her husband was not the father of the child. This story is but a symbol of the hurried, savorless conjugal relations that are the only kind allowed for the multiplication of mankind.

How they would have crossed themselves in terror, those sourly devout old women who, under the mask of ardent piety, beg heaven to help them out in the petty crimes they commit in the name of virtue, in their saintly efforts at home-wrecking, in their perfidious schemes to break off or speed up an inheritance!

Imagine the terror of the young faithful who, scarcely washed of their daily foibles, were already trembling with fresh guilt at the prospect of an afternoon rendezvous!

Think of the healthy, superior contempt emanating from grown men who that same morning had just left the bawdy houses of the neighboring town!

Blessed are the poor in spirit! Sure of themselves and proud of their actions, they fulfill their destiny in total smugness, knowing neither doubt nor remorse.

13

By the time we returned to our box our group had forgotten the stage action and were chatting, laughing and joking with the *hsiang-k'ung* who had come over to greet us.

Wang ordered drinks, pastries and a few select dishes; the dinner began all over again. Precious Treasure, having finished his toilette, joined us as soon as he was sure his protector had left. Curious about his present life, I asked him where he lived.

"At Chang's house. I mean the house where he used to live, since he has now abandoned us for his jewel. And very glad of it we are."

"Why?"

"First of all because right now he is in trouble and might be nasty. This way we are spared his beatings when we go to a banquet and fail to bring back money."

"How could that come about?" I asked incredulously.

"It happened to me the day before yesterday. Not only did I come home empty-handed, but I had to spend a little money myself."

The guests stopped chattering to listen to us. The boy told how, at the end of the show, he had passed a table where three young scholars were conversing with a *wu-shêng*. They had stopped Precious Treasure and made him sit down. Invited to supper, he accompanied them to the Three Joys restaurant.

They snuggled into a private room on the second floor, and as the hosts did not seem overly prosperous, extravagant dishes were not ordered.

He had noticed at once that the three young men knew nothing about life. The classics teach us little about the etiquette of amorous relationships. Their manners were strangely daring considering that they were in public, but they blushed unexpectedly at the mildest joke. Precious Treasure perfidiously amused himself by teaching them gestures and actions which later on could not fail to involve them in the worst difficulties.

Our entire group burst into laughter when he did a take-off on his own proceedings. He showed us how the naive young man, upon his instruction, had taken him on his knees, slipped his hand inside his own robe and pulled his breeches down from his belt, ready right then and there to satisfy his sexual appetite . . . in front of all his friends and in a public place! Meanwhile, Precious Treasure had signaled to the other *hsiang-k'ung,* who, when he heard footsteps in the hall, immediately threw the door open. At that moment the rascally clown got up suddenly, exposing the undraped young man, half-dead from embarrassment, to the full view of the passers-by, who all began shrieking with laughter.

When the dinner party was over, the waiter brought the bill, which totaled more than eight strings of cash. The oldest of the youths had confidently thrust his hand into an inside pocket of his robe and drawn it out empty. His expression changed. He arose, fumbling in his belt, unbuttoning and searching his inside pocket once more. Zero. His comrades looked dismayed and asked him:

"Have you lost our leather purse?"

"So it seems. Are you sure none of you has it?"

While his two companions fumbled through their pockets and belts, the waiter, who had been watching them with sarcastic expression, finally said:

"Don't waste your time looking any further; you won't find anything. I've been working here ten years and I'm very familiar with this old dodge. Every day customers tell us they've lost their purses and that they mean to return the following day. But we never allow them to leave until they pay up."

The group protested indignantly. The waiter shook his head and went on.

"There are three of you. Let one of you run home and pick up the money. I'll warn the doorman not to let the other two leave."

When the waiter left, the three young men looked at each other in consternation. Precious Treasure, knowing their naiveté, had the impression they were honest, so he questioned them. The oldest confessed that, having wanted to attend the theater with his cousins, and not having the wherewithal, he had taken advantage of a moment of his father's inattentiveness to filch a twelve-ounce silver ingot from a coffer that had been left open. He had hidden the loot in a leather purse and placed it carefully in an inside pocket of his robe, where he had touched it occasionally while he was seated in the theater. Where and how had he lost it? As for asking his parents for the money, he would not dare. He felt certain they would refuse, and they might even give him a thrashing.

Precious Treasure then recalled that on leaving the theater he had seen the young man trip over an invisible obstacle and fall. A passer-by had tried to keep him from falling but without success, then had helped him up and dusted him off rather too assiduously, he remembered. That overly solicitous passer-by had doubtless provoked the fall in order to pick his victim's pocket.

Meanwhile, what to do? The relatives of the three young men would certainly not help out, and the restaurant owner would be adamant. The young men, crushed, had then asked their little friends to forgive them for not being able to give them a customary token of esteem. The second *hsiang-k'ung* had replied gently:

"It does not matter. We had a good laugh and I am very happy."

But Precious Treasure knew how exacting the poor child's master was and how he beat him unmercifully if he did not bring him several ounces of silver every night.

At that moment all the guests began to laugh at the story and to recount similar adventures to one another. But I was still interested, so I asked Precious Treasure what had happened. He answered with annoyance.

"It got straightened out by itself."

Seeing that I wanted to know and no one was listening, he said to me rapidly in a low voice:

"You are a foreigner. I trust you. Don't repeat a word of this. I was sorry for my friend and our hosts, and told them I would try to get help from some of my own friends in the restaurant. Leaving the room I ran to a dark corner and pried a ten-ounce bill out of the lining of my robe."

"Out of the lining of your robe?" I cried out surprised.

"Sh! . . . Yes. That's my hiding place for the money I manage to hold back from the *shih fu*. He hasn't discovered it yet."

"Have the young men returned your ten ounces?"

"Not yet. It's a large sum. They need time."

At first impulse I started to draw a bill out of my wallet. A slightly sneering expression on Precious Treasure's face stopped me short. The story had been nothing but a clever invention trumped up to get a present. The other guests had been on to it long before. That was why they had changed the subject before the fable had ended.

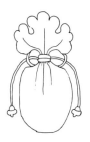

14

While returning in the peaceful night I began to wonder whether Minister Yüan knew anything about the information that Precious Treasure had involuntarily given concerning Pei Yu's abductor. Being unsure, I thought it best to advise the old gentleman. Therefore I ordered my servant to present my card to the Minister as soon as dawn had broken and to give him the message personally and in secret. Letters go astray and are difficult to disclaim.

But at the mention of the Beileh Fan the steward exclaimed:

"The cook just happens to have a cousin who is a gardener at Fan's palace. We shall find out everything from him. I can make inquiries. The Great Man would do better to wait."

With my permission, early the following morning my servant brought in the cook accompanied by a white-haired old man whose face was a mass of wrinkles and deeply tanned. The cook presented his cousin, then withdrew at his colleague's imperious gesture, while the gardener finished his greetings.

"You work at the palace of the Beileh Fan?" I asked.

"I am his slave, but I am not in the palace," he answered.

"What do you mean?" I insisted uneasily. "Aren't you his gardener?"

"Yes, yes. But not at his palace. I take care of one of his gardens in the Outer City."

"Then he knows nothing," I said to my majordomo with a sigh

of disappointment.

However, my man broke into a broad smile and shook his head.

"On the contrary. He knows everything. The *hsiang-k'ung* is shut up in this flower garden."

The gardener was also smiling.

"Have you seen Pei Yu?" I asked. "Are you sure it is he?"

Assisted by my servant I grilled him, and he told me that since his abduction, Pei Yu had been shut up in a room whose windows gave on to the garden. The old man had been struck by his extreme beauty as well as by his sadness. He then questioned the servants and learned that Prince Li's men were the real culprits. At that moment they were expecting the Prince himself to arrive.

"The Prince?" I interrupted. "But he has been gone for ten or twelve days at least!"

"Then the Great Man does not know," answered the steward, "that high magistrates reporting to a distant post often allow their retinue to precede them slowly, while they themselves hide in a friend's country house. There they wait for news from the Court. Intrigues might develop quite rapidly against a courtier who has just left the city. If danger really exists, the absentee may return under one pretext or another to direct his own defense. If, on the other hand, the envious have made no headway against him, the newly promoted official can peacefully continue on his way."

The gardener then went on to say that actually Prince Li had arrived the evening before. Fan had immediately prepared a banquet and had then withdrawn early to leave the couple alone together.

The old man, who was something of a voyeur, had remained in the garden unnoticed. As soon as it grew dark enough to conceal his movements, he glided under the windows. Then, by wetting the translucent paper covering the windows with the tip of his finger, he had been able to tear it noiselessly with his sharpest fingernail and make a hole just big enough to watch through without being seen.

The Manchu was already alone with Pei Yu. Half-slumped over the table, his face flushed with wine and wrath, he berated the boy.

"Who do you think you are, miserable insect," he shouted, "to dare resist my advances? To be able to defy me, you must count on

Yüan's power. Where is that power now and can it keep me from
doing whatever I want with you? Speak! Answer me! What do you
want from me? A palace? Slaves? I shall have your master killed if he
refuses to release you. . . Do you want gems? Pearls?"

But the boy remained impassive. As the old voyeur expressed it,
you could feel that he would not have sold the shadow of a smile even
for a bushel basket filled with gold dust. The Prince, by then boiling
over with fury, had threatened to kill him. Pei Yu had answered sadly:

"You may do as you like with my body. I haven't the strength to
resist you. But you want something else from me. Do you believe
that by using force you will obtain anything more than a cadaver? Do
you not know that the most sumptuous gifts have never bought anything more than lukewarm friendship? True love is only acquired
through feeling, and you do not love me since you are obliged to use
force . . . But watch out! Minister Yüan is powerful. Who knows if
his emissaries do not already have us under surveillance, waiting for a
chance to bring about your downfall."

Then the kidnaper, in confusion, had wheeled around with such
glowering rage that the old gardener had quickly taken his eye away
from the hole, certain that he had been noticed and expecting to be
beaten to death.

But the argument had only begun all over again and the old man,
reassured now that he was unnoticed, had seen the Prince take Pei Yu
by the hand . . . a white hand, slender and supple as though it were
boneless, as the old one expressed it. A lotus bud ready to burst into
full bloom. He drew him toward the ebony bed encrusted with
rainbow-colored mother-of-pearl, where the rose light of silken
lanterns threw a dawn-like blush on the child's pale face.

"All right," said the Manchu with a chuckle. "I'll attempt to win
your love, since it turns out that a Minister of Imperial Blood must
demean himself to flatter one of his vilest subjects."

With a rough hand he tried to caress the flower-like countenance,
but when confronted by the *hsiang-k'ung*'s instinctive recoil, he grew
furious once again. Shouting a thousand insults, he knocked the child
down and tore his robe.

The gardener at this point had become so carried away, so moved by compassion, and by another emotion as well, I should judge, that he leaned heavily against the window. The weak frame trembled and cracked apart.

The Prince turned around suddenly, saw the broken window and immediately called out at the top of his voice. Looking for a weapon, he snatched up a bronze tripod and flailed it around like a club, storming outside and directing the search as his guards rushed in.

Meanwhile the old man, terror-struck by his own indiscretion, fled without losing a second. Knowing the garden thoroughly, he had reached a secret door that opened onto a dark alley running alongside the close long before anyone could see him.

After wandering around for a while in the deserted streets not knowing what to do, he had come back toward the Main Gate. Near there he was joined by a breathless servant who cried out:

"Have you seen him?"

The prudent gardener answered, "No. What about you? Have you seen anything?"

And accompanying the man, he had reached the portico where guards were shouting and gesticulating. Some of them said that the intruders numbered at least a hundred and that they had scaled the walls like cats. Others stated that the Prince had put up a stiff fight, but that, overwhelmed by their number, he had been forced to let them take the *hsiang-k'ung*.

Thus he learned that the child had disappeared in the tumult. Had he fled? Terrified, had he perhaps thrown himself into a well?

15

I was now totally in the dark as to what had befallen Pei Yu. The first thing to do was to hang on to some tangible clue from this strange adventure. If the gardener, still shaken by the previous night's emotion, had blabbed everything in the morning, doubtless he would soon recover the prudent silence of civilized man. Once he was sure that no one had seen him in the gardens, he would deny everything in order to avoid complications.

So my majordomo rapidly wrote up a detailed account of the evening, noting with care all the gardener's given names, his age and place of birth. Then he prepared a little ink stamp and, following a Chinese custom for important documents that goes back to time immemorial, he required him to affix his thumb print at the end of the account. The gardener hesitated, trying to avoid committing himself. The sight of a few silver ingots and the promise that we would allow him to escape before we made use of his testimony, made up his mind for him. After we pointed out to him the danger of any indiscretion, we had him taken back to his distant quarter.

Armed with the critical document, I proceeded in haste to the Minister's palace. I hoped to catch him between his return from the dawn audience and his departure for the Cabinet council.

While in my cart in front of his office, as my card was being presented according to custom, I reflected that many hours had passed since Pei Yu's disappearance. Where was he now? Was he still alive?

The customary announcement of "*Ch'ing*," that is, "If you please," roused me from my troubled reflections. The steward of the palace led me into a side pavilion, the library where, on the shelves of a bookcase with red highlights, the scrolls were piled up, horizontally, each one with a little tag that bore its title.

I had scarcely had time to admire a splendid Thirteenth Century work when the Minister entered, affable, showing neither by look nor intonation the astonishment that my arrival at this hour must have caused him, nor even any curiosity as to the reason for this early-morning intrusion—even though I felt as if I were conducting myself with an indecorous haste. I abandoned all pretense of a visit made for the sole pleasure of bestowing my presence. As soon as he had signaled to his servants to withdraw, I immediately handed him the gardener's deposition and described what he had told me and what I had done.

He listened with a serious mien, assenting slightly with a nod or two. Then he read the document attentively and murmured in a tone of satisfaction:

"An important paper, which I could never have obtained by myself. The witnesses are all above suspicion."

He then slipped the deposition into the top of his silken boot. Smiling, he took my hand and patted it softly.

"From the first day I met you, I felt that your happy influence would caress my life with a favorable breeze . . . First of all I want to reassure you. Our friend is in my palace. I, too, knew what was going on at the Beileh's flower garden. I was waiting, however, for the real kidnaper to compromise himself before returning the prisoner."

"How could you have acted soon enough to stop that beastly lout from committing an outrage on the child?"

"At the first outcry, they would have broken down the door and arrested him. Only dogs in heat disport themselves in public."

"Yes, but the Prince could not possibly be tried for kidnap and rape of a *hsiang-k'ung*. I assume nothing can be done about him?"

The courtier smiled subtly.

"Legal punishments are for stupid commoners. The nobles can be gotten at by other methods. This very morning the Prince's attempt and failure were obligingly whispered into the sacred ear of the Lord-of-Ten-Thousand-Years. One of the 'old rooster' guards attached to the Imperial staff told him the whole story at the beginning of the audience. Who would have imagined it? The August Emperor furrowed his dragon's brow deeply. At the same moment, behind the carved screen encircling the Throne, the Dowager Empress, our 'Old Buddha,' nervously clicked her bracelets. Her imperious voice could be heard ordering one of the palace guards to overtake Prince Li and to accompany him, to travel with him day and night until he reached his distant Vice-realm. Pei Yu has nothing more to fear. Day after tomorrow, for the Feast of Lanterns, he has invited several friends into my gardens. I should be happy to receive you then. Please come at nightfall."

As he seemed to have nothing more to say, I slowly stretched out my hand toward one of the two tea cups perched between us on the long, narrow, multicolored lacquer chow bench, whose sculptured and rounded feet seemed to be genuflecting on the thin mattress upholstered in scarlet silk that covered the divan. He duplicated my gesture. I was free to leave.

16

In spring the Feast of Lanterns falls on the fifteenth night of the first moon, and celebrates the final victory of the sun over the dragons of darkness. Formerly it was the most joyous of public ceremonies. Everyone, great or small, went out into the throng-filled streets when night fell, carrying some frail, fantastic luminous replica of an animal, flower or object of favorable omen. It was truly a contest of grace and fantasy to make mythological figures real: the bat, whose name also signifies happiness and the very sight of which constitutes a mystical appeal to invisible chance; peaches that bestow immortality; a bluebird who announces the arrival of Hsi-Wang-Mu, sorceress and goddess of beauty; a three-legged cock who lives on the sun; a white hare who brews love potions and whose prototype resides in the moon; a sunflower with countless seeds, symbol of fertility.

Nevertheless, from year to year, the winds of mocking disbelief that fog over the entire globe, increasingly separating mankind from nature, manage to weaken this expression of simple and spontaneous joy that comes at the release from the long winter nights. Nowadays it is only in a few out-of-the-way towns that these celebrations spill out into the streets rather than remaining confined within the family.

On that particular evening, while proceeding along the city's wide thoroughfares which were always dark because the penny-pinching government left the task of street lighting to the care of the citizens, we met only a few groups of small children who were singing and running about, dangling their modest lanterns from the ends of long bamboo poles.

In front of the entrance of the Minister's gardens innumerable lanterns traced a sparkling triumphal archway and, as we moved along the brown and yellow "tiger skin" pattern stone wall, the intermittent explosions of firecrackers and the sputtering of rockets ripped through the nighttime silence.

A crowd of rather elegant gentlemen was gathered at the entry, immobile and seemingly waiting for something to happen. I was wondering what those scholars were doing there when suddenly amid a general buzz of satisfaction, eight giant all-white lanterns, each one bearing a string of ideograms, rose up slowly under the luminous archway.

A rumble broke our immediately and swelled through the crowd as they read aloud. There followed discussions and laughter. The spectators had been brought together for the ancient game of *teng-mi,* the "lantern riddles." On the vast, white spheres each column of ideograms paraphrased a verse of a well-known poem that had to be reconstructed.

The first person to guess correctly would have his name announced with fanfare and would receive a prize. Thus, those who thought they had found the answers could be seen speedily detaching themselves from the group.

Under the portico, was enthroned a high-ranking magistrate in robes embroidered with the insignia of his rank, wearing the sapphire button of imperial favor on his fur bonnet. He listened to the scholars carefully, but frequently smiled and shook his head: the answer was wrong.

I should have liked to stay around to learn the results of this difficult competition. My majordomo decided differently and announced me. A steward approached and led me across the entry court toward the pavilion where the master received his guests.

The nocturnal gardens were still bare from the winter gone by. But a softness in the light evening air announced the arrival of spring. Already the first blades of grass could be seen in the multicolored lines of lantern light bordering the alleyways. Already the limp little willow branches were burgeoning.

Behind a dark mass of majestic cedars, an enchanting vision suddenly took form. A forest of peach trees with lustrous flowers bloomed in the night. A mist enveloped the perfumed brilliance of the delicate petals subtly lighted by thousands of tiny lanterns.

The alley, twisting and turning beneath the rosy light, soon ended by skirting a little mirror lake in which the lighted peach trees were reflected upside down, together with the strange rocks of the lake's shores and a pavilion that appeared to rest on upturned roof corners, showing off its complicated silhouette and its glass windows lighted scarlet, orange and bright blue. The snowy whiteness of a sculptured marble terrace and balustrade supported by dark red pilings united the inverted image with the real edifice.

On these snowy steps the Minister, alone, clad in a robe of periwinkle silk lined with white fox, awaited me, shaking his two clasped hands in an amicable sign of welcome. Scarcely had I bowed to him when he took me by the hand. Then, with a finger to his lips, he drew me to the rear of the pavilion. A door stood open.

He had me enter a room whose darkness was relieved only by the soft lights from the peach trees framed by the doorway. Once there he drew close to my ear and whispered:

"For a long time I have noticed that you did not at all understand our feelings about the *hsiang-k'ung*. Today I am going to let you witness a difficult double test. Look through the transparent pane of this window. We are going to observe everything that goes on in the neighboring room without being seen."

Two chairs were placed under the window. He led me there and sat down himself, adding in a low voice.

"I must explain this to you. A young scholar named Jui Hsing, Star-of-Wisdom, had been passing his entire day before our friend's door, watching him as he got into his carriage to leave. Then he would wait for his return, but never make any attempt to get to know him, nor be received. When Pei Yu disappeared, Star-of-Wisdom's despair drew my servant's attention and this silent love intrigued me. That the young scholar had received top honors in the recent high examinations was well known. In spite of his talents, however, he despaired for his future since he was possessed of neither fortune nor influence. Pei Yu, when I spoke of him, said he had noticed him and on my recommendation has invited him for this evening. I have made up my mind, though, to test his character before giving him my protection. I arranged to have our friend receive him here in the next room where they believe themselves alone."

My silence must have smacked of disapproval, for he continued:

"I can read your mind, and I, too, think it is neither delicate nor loyal to try to surprise the intimate thoughts of those we love. There is, however, no other way to verify feelings, to distinguish clearly the pure from the impure. You see, I want to assure myself that the sparkling diamond of these two souls is truly flawless. For if Star-of-Wisdom loves our friend unreservedly, our friend has also been deeply touched by this silent homage. How will Pei Yu receive him? Ah! My child, profit well by the charm of your youth. For youth feels passion for youth and can give age nothing more than admiration and respect."

He interrupted himself and gripped my hand to impress silence and attention. Sure enough, in the neighboring room a graceful adolescent had entered. One whose pure origins were attested to by his fair skin, fine profile and large black eyes with thick eyelashes.

A few moments later, through the soft shadows of the dimly lit room entered Pei Yu.

The adolescent, who had been seated on the divan, got up quickly and stood speechless, blushing wildly, his large eyes fixed on the charming silhouette. To use a traditional expression, all the flowers of his heart bloomed on his face.

The *hsiang-k'ung,* also immobile, smiled sweetly without speaking. Curious lights that I had never seen before flitted from his glance. Finally, in his musical voice, he pronounced the customary greeting:

"For a long while, with my eyes turned to heaven, I have awaited your visit."

Advancing, he took the visitor's hand and made him sit down next to him on the divan where a squat milk-glass lamp cast its pale glow into the two troubled faces that were turned toward one another.

One felt that Star-of-Wisdom could neither bring himself to clasp the hand that held his own nor to let it go. A deep feeling of timidity or of modesty had overcome him. Pei Yu continued:

"Was it to catch sight of me that you have been standing like that in front of my house? Then the red cord which the God of Unions uses to bind our two souls is already that strong?"

In a shaky voice the visitor replied, "I acknowledge my indiscretion and beg you to forgive me."

"But why have you waited so long to pay your respects? The days have gone by. My eyes must have told you my desire to make your acquaintance."

"I heard about your pride. You refuse to receive any visitors . . . who was I, without fortune or rank, to dare disturb you?"

"Were your feelings so weak that a passing rumor could hold them in check? Look into my eyes. Do they belong to a cold egotist with a heart of stone?"

Leaning on Star-of-Wisdom's shoulder he raised his eyes toward him and drew his face closer and closer, smiling with vermilion lips.

The visitor looked dazed. He trembled slightly and paled. Then the *hsiang-k'ung* threw himself on the youngster's chest, clasping him in his arms, his face all steamy with sensuality.

17

During this scene my neighbor squeezed my hand violently. He murmured to himself, "Will he yield? Is he like snow melting at the first sunshine? Or shall we see the priceless jade that I have assumed he was made of?"

In spite of myself I blurted, "Actually, Star-of-Wisdom is the only worthy one of the two. Who would have thought that Pei Yu would sway like a willow . . . ?"

The old gentleman whispered into my ear, "You are overcome with astonishment and indignation. However, refrain from pronouncing judgment. It will prevent you from fully tasting the exquisite agony of your feelings. Do not try, as you are now doing, to suppress your deepest emotions. On the contrary, develop them and refine them still more. The time will arrive all too soon when your capability for feeling emotion will weaken entirely—when in the desert of your senile boredom, searching in vain for the oasis of an unadulterated thrill, you cry aloud into the void. . ."

The emotion that had been shaking the adolescent's frame suddenly seemed to dissipate. Gently disengaging himself from his host's embrace, he got up and said in a still shaky voice that grew more and more steady:

"What is sweetest in the invisible ties attaching one human being to another is the assurance of being known and understood beneath the deceptive mask of word and gesture. Your attitude towards me proves

that you are still ignorant of my deepest nature. You judge me badly.
It is true that unreasonable emotions animate me. But please understand that my reason is always in control—"

"Nevertheless—" interrupted the *hsiang-k'ung.*

But the youth did not allow him to explain. He continued, "The
kind of relations you propose bring pleasures that are too fleeting. If I
gave them leeway, they would rob me of the emotions arising from
your heart and spirit that would grow better and richer each day."

Pei Yu answered as if surprised, "Is it not true that human beings
who love one another are attached physically as well as spiritually?
Why abandon bodily pleasures in favor of the heart and intellect
alone?"

"Physical pleasure ought to be the inevitable consequence, not
the point of departure of a love affair. Meng-Tse said as much twenty-
three centuries ago. The heart and spirit are to the body what the
cutting edge is to the blade. Little matters it that a saber be encrusted
with gold; if the cutting edge is not of fine steel, it is worthless as a
saber. One would go better armed with a heavy bludgeon."

By the feeble light that crossed our window, I perceived the
Minister's face. His fine features were beaming with an intense joy, a
joy made up of diverse elements but wherein I could distinguish the
enthusiasm of a collector before an object of extreme rarity, the happy
satisfaction of an artist who has just finished a masterpiece, the transports of a theater lover before a perfect and thrilling scene, the
passionate respect for the noblest forms of virtue . . . and who can say
what besides? The icy desert of his decline contained many oases of
fertility.

He finally murmured, "Star-of-Wisdom is worthy of the highest
posts in the realm. Whoever is able to use reason to dominate his most

violent passions is capable of undying resistance to the countless temptations that cross the paths of magistrates weighed down by responsibility. As for Pei Yu, have no fear. He played the seduction scene from *Nocturnal Encounter* like the incomparable artist I know him to be."

Glancing back into the neighboring room I remained speechless at the child's transfiguration. His disturbing amorous expression was gone. He had reassumed his natural look of sweet modesty and seriousness. Advancing toward his guest he knelt and struck his head on the thick carpet, exclaiming:

"I beseech you to pardon my crime, even though I deserve death."

And when the adolescent, recovered from his surprise, pulled him up, with a melancholy air Pei Yu added:

"We *hsiang-k'ung* are instruments of pleasure and find it hard to believe in the rectitude of those who pursue us. I wanted to test your heart on the touchstone of wantonness to make certain that the gold of your love was pure. I am now convinced that your loyalty is unqualified. But alas! I also fear that I have wrecked my own image in your eyes . . . that I have cast the disquieting poison of doubt into your spotless soul . . ."

In Star-of-Wisdom's clear and penetrating gaze could be read the double question: Was he sincere just now? Or is this new performance entirely put on?

Doubtless the scholar read the truth in the sad, sweet eyes of his questioner, for a slightly serious smile lit up his face. Then he took Pei Yu by the hand and bade him sit down on the divan again, saying:

"By the courage you displayed in the playing of this role that was far beneath you, I measure the sentiments that you must have for me and likewise those you expect of me. I hope you will not be disappointed."

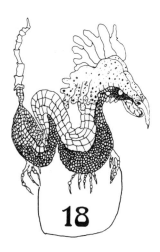

18

The old Minister, standing next to me, allowed the curtain to fall over the transparent window. Getting up noiselessly, he gently led me outside the pavilion.

"Let us leave them alone and rejoin our guests in the gardens. The double test was conclusive. Their charming friendship reminds me of the time when I, too, having come to the capital without favor or fortune, had nevertheless managed to place among the first in the Official Examinations. A government post was slow in arriving, however. And in my poverty, I often went to sleep at night without having eaten a single meal during the day. Alone, I gradually lost hope despite four faithful, lifelong friends."

"Alone and poverty stricken," I exclaimed, "Despite four faithful friends?"

"These four best friends of the sensitive man are the setting sun, moonlight, the first flower of spring and a warm summer breeze. They make up for every heartache, but they can scarcely nourish us. In spite of their help I was going to renounce any aspiration toward an official career and accept some modest employment as an accountant or a teacher, when as fate would have it, I met a young actor. A succession of disasters had caused the ruin and death of his father, governor of the district. He had then been abandoned to the care of a relative, also a scholar, but who had been forced to accept employment in a theater in order to survive. His birth and gifts had been ignored, and they only thought of making a singer of him. But his soul had kept the nobility of the Sacred Doctrine, the moral code we were all taught by Confucius. In his attachment to me, he was distressed to see my future compromised in this way. He helped me by giving me countless gifts, sustaining me by his counsels and his affection. Thanks to him alone I was able to obtain a post and as a result I really owe to him the high office that the Supreme Benevolence has bestowed on me."

He stopped speaking. Curiosity opened my lips. I asked:

"What happened to this lofty soul?"

We were on the snowy terrace in a luminous white and rose mist illumined by the peach tree's lighted blossoms. Even in this faint light I could see a dark cloud pass over the old gentleman's face. He sighed sorrowfully:

"In my tender, grateful love, I knew no happiness except being near him. This became the subject of a thousand calumnies from those envious of my already rapid rise to fortune. I was accused of neglecting my duties in favor of pleasure. The scandal was great. Persons who wished me well informed my friend. The letter he wrote me that same day weighs forever on my heart.

"'Only one course is left,' he wrote, 'to obliterate the dangers our friendship throws in the path of your future. I can only beg you to forgive me the sadness my death will cause you . . .'"

We were interrupted by a great burst of explosions. The last fireworks were crackling now, reproducing conflagrations of ancient palaces, attacks on citadels with crumbling walls agape where they had been torn apart by mines, the ascension of the Immortals and Sages on many-colored clouds.

Now from different corners of the garden, dragons of five colors, symbolizing the power of Darkness and the clouds of winter, unwound their giant coils and bounded forth while opening and closing their jaws and spurting flames, pursuing the Sun's immense red ball as he escaped on his annual flight.

Suddenly, in a simultaneous blast, thousands of rockets blossomed in the sky, creating a brightness stronger than daylight. The victory of the Orb of Day was assured.

When the heavens grew dark and my gaze fell back to earth once more, the dragons had disappeared. In the returning obscurity, only the forest of peach trees, symbol of love, went on flowering, softly luminous in the pure calm of the moving springtime night.

19

For several years after this, destiny kept me away from the capital. On returning from this exile I remembered the counsels of Minister Yüan and immediately reserved a place in the theater where Pei Yu was supposed to give a matinee that very day.

Happy to be back in Peking, I left early in order to be able to stroll to the theater district. My first walk in the city had plenty of unexpected surprises.

The least agreeable change was the cold, even hostile, attitude of the small merchants and of the populace. The very same booksellers who formerly greeted me with thousands of courteous attentions, today would not unbend in the slightest unless they saw that we were alone.

Street urchins, who ran by and shouted *"Ma-ni, yang kuei tzu!"*—"Damn you, foreign devil!"—before disappearing around the corner, certainly reflected their parents' thinking. They no longer followed me in silent, amused bands laughing to themselves and making fun of my absurd clothes and my strange occidental bearing.

The Europeans, enshrouded in their own impenetrable ignorance of the country, of its customs and language, treated me as a fanciful dreamer and a pessimist when, in the following days, I made known my observations. Only the learned and well-informed missionaries were troubled by this growing hostility.

Another surprise was to observe the changes that had come to theater posters. Hardly visible before I left, they now stretched out extensively on all the walls next to ads that extolled: here, a surgeon's needle useful for making inopportune pregnancies disappear; there, a reputable pharmacist's infallible pills for the same purpose; and over there, irresistible silk stuffs recently arrived at a suburban merchant's from Kwantung.

At the top of one of the theater posters Pei Yu's name leapt to the eye, written in a red square on yellow paper in fat, high characters. I was amused to notice that the name placed at the bottom of the poster, and given equal lettering according to the "English star system," was that of the jealous clown, Precious Treasure.

That day a gory drama called "Jade Screen Mountain" was to be performed. Pei Yu was playing the heroine, P'an Chao-yun, with a mysterious seductiveness that took away from the role all the hatefulness the unknown author had written into it.

Deceiving her husband with a young priest, she is lectured in vain by her old and ridiculous father. Discovered by her husband's blood-brother, the virtuous Shih Hsiu, she then has him driven from the house. Wordlessly, while finishing her coiffure to the antique tones of the leitmotiv played in all operas during a lady's toilette, she succeeds, by using a few glances and graceful poses before her mirror, in driving her poor husband frantic with love and jealousy. Shih Hsiu comes back that night, kills the priest and goes to inform her husband. But once again in her presence, her husband cannot bring himself to harm her. Then Shih Hsiu cuts off her head and that of her attendant and accomplice Ying-êrh.

The entire hall, gasping with anxiety for the beauty, groaned over her sad fate rather than admiring the virtuous action of the executioner. A cloud of admiration, desire and love rose from the pit. The rasping bravos and applause seemed akin to the cries of cats in the night.

Thus Pei Yu, from his fame as a *hsiang-k'ung,* had risen to the still rarer eminence of illustrious singer. He must have been about 16 years old by then. He had made the forbidding transition to puberty without his voice cracking in the manner suffered by most adolescents, making them forever unacceptable in feminine roles.

I understood the lyric note of the reviewers in all the dailies I had read. It was not simply physical attraction that was responsible for such articles as that of the theater critic in the *Jih Pao:*

". . . How can I acclaim this strange and rare talent enough, those pure notes rising to the sky, so like the twelve jade arrows from the crystal pavilions that the Goddess of Beauty, Hsi-Wang-Mu, had constructed around her aerial palace in the Jasper City. Those modulations more enchanting than the song of the amorous phoenix in the Isles of the Genies, that beauty, finally, which ravishes the soul at one fell swoop, and carries it off to the eastern reaches of Beatitude."

20

It was an unpleasant thought after such a long separation to have to see Pei Yu once more in the overheated atmosphere of the backstage area, to exchange our first words while being spied on and jostled. I sent to ask when he could receive me. My servant informed me that I would be expected immediately at the adolescent's new house, at the Duck's Bill Crossing beyond Eternal Peace Avenue.

To the clip-clop trot of the mule, the carriage traversed the long, silent way, plunging into peaceful, obscure little streets and finally depositing me in front of a narrow vermilion door whose freshly painted wood and heavy brass knocker with polished highlights glistered softly by the light of our carriage lamp.

The porter, undoubtedly expecting us, opened the door even before we had a chance to knock. He looked us over carefully, however, before we were admitted to the courtyard. His giant proportions and the enormous cudgel dangling from his belt left few doubts as to the reception in store for us if we had tried to enter uninvited.

Within the close, the usual arrangement. First a little courtyard, then a portico. Then a second court surrounded by verandas, bedecked with flowers and large porcelain tanks where swam goldfish with multiple tails. Gnarled pine trees rose high above the roof tops, twisting their branches in silhouette against the starry heavens.

A door opened to a lighted room . . . Pei Yu's elegant silhouette on the threshold . . . a young man now, serious, conscious of his immense celebrity as well as of the constant adoration that surrounds him. Almost majestic, so quickly does the habit of being respected show itself in our attitudes.

The familiar form of address no longer came to my lips. But he, aware of custom, knelt down. And as I lifted him up he squeezed my hands for a long while repeating the traditional words with apparent sincerity.

"I have truly suffered from our overlong separation. That makes me all the more happy to see you."

Troubled, I felt a strange question grow within me. Was he a boy or a young girl, this fragile offspring of an ancient race?

He was already leading me toward the divan where stood a young man I recognized; it was he whom I had spied upon several years ago through an indiscreet window. His robe of puce-colored silk lined with pale blue and a bonnet crowned with a sapphire button left no doubt as to his rapid rise to fortune.

Pei Yu, encircling him with his slender arms, introduced him in a cajoling manner.

"You two must not be jealous of one another. He is my dear brother, you will always be the well-meaning genie without whose aid my destiny—our destiny—could never have been fulfilled."

Making me lie on the bright-colored silks, he sat down on the other side of the low table against the knees of his reclining friend.

While my lips and my ears followed the affectionate modulations of the conversation, my spirit, detached, bathed with a restless curiosity in the emanations hovering around the deep feeling, rare and indefinable, that bound these two together—a feeling free from all sordid thought, made up of whole devotion, of admiration and of mutual respect. Dare I say pure? Well, yes, pure. It was that far above any beastly preoccupations. They were far removed from the contempt that any depraved person feels for his associate.

Pei Yu's life had grown increasingly free. His master, while withholding the larger part of his earnings, nevertheless allowed him enough so that he could taste the joys of having about him art objects, flowers, sumptuous silks, so that he could live at last in an atmosphere of ease and beauty.

When they called him now for an evening it was no longer for the purpose of troubling guests with the equivocal caresses of the *hsiang-k'ung,* but in order to hear him sing an act from his repertoire and to have him join literary jousts with enthusiasts whose feelings were still expressed in burning glances but whose compliments were couched in elaborate forms, masking with poetry their overardent thoughts.

Life at Court was, however, changing rapidly and dangerously. A certain Prince Tuan, a brutal and vulgar Manchu, had gained an inexplicable control over the Empress Dowager. Just as bad money drives out good, he was little by little chasing sensitive and reasonable scholars from the capital. Those who could see ahead were already accusing him of preparing a coup d'état for his own ends. He was also considered dangerous because, under the pretext of checking the invasion of foreigners who had talked openly of "slicing up the cake," he encouraged the mystical exercises of the para-military secret society called *I-Ho Ch'üan*, "Fists of Justice and Harmony," whose members thought themselves, thanks to their magic formulas, invulnerable to bullets and swords.

Our planet, in its course though space, had perhaps entered into a celestial region impregnated with a subtle poison which had penetrated our atmosphere. Indeed, it was a time when throughout the entire world nations were constantly increasing their armies and were beginning to look around for trouble. Humanity's Reason was already beclouded by a madness that later would set fire to the entire world.

But in the gentle shadow of the divan, the two friends indulged me with elegant and harmonious conversation. Their subtle minds, honed by music, poetry, literature and art, never had been occupied by worldly ambition or jealous struggle, with the petty and mundane. They were, however, in direct and frequent contact with those who manipulated people for their own interests, and they painfully perceived the arrival of a period of bloody brutality, of a collapse of civilization all over the world. Both of them, raising toward the future's menacing darkness the feeble rays of their logical intuition, showed me how the hideous monsters of Pillage, Murder, Rape, Fire and Destruction lurked in the shadows.

The prophets, alas! see the danger threatening the world better than those who, themselves, will be its next victims.

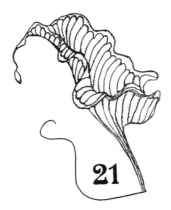

21

Truly the world had changed and strange news was being told on all sides. Our old enemy, Prince Li, had returned more powerful than ever. First cousin of Prince Tuan, he had all the favor and sympathy of this new dictator and could give free rein to his brutal imagination.

At dinner, my neighbor told me that Li had brought a singular instrument from the South, a heavy box that could be fixed solidly to the divan and, being lacquered, ornamented and gilded, replaced the high table with twisted feet that was usually placed in the midst of the great couch.

When a chosen guest arrived, the host took him to the place of honor; he made him sit down by the instrument on which had already been placed the ritual teacup that one is supposed to take with both hands. Who could suspect treachery? The visitor, however, lifting the cup, released a secret spring. Suddenly, with the speed of lightning, a pair of steel handcuffs sprang shut on the wrists of the unfortunate guest, who was in this way rendered defenseless to his host's every whim.

Keeping my feelings under control, for I did not know whether the narrator might not be a friend of the "beast," I said simply:

"Since the trap is now known, very few birds must be taken."

He smiled knowingly.

"With your occidental rectitude you do not take human nature into account. Those who are caught never brag about it, you may be sure. Many of them, so as not to be the only ones undergoing the adventure, send acquaintances to be entrapped. Among the persons who have heard of the trap there are those who feign ignorance in order to be caught, hoping by tears or threats to obtain a goodly sum from their host."

"Those are the ones," I interposed without being able to check myself, "who get a bad reception. No doubt they receive more blows than money."

"Exactly," my neighbor replied calmly.

"And this trap has never caused its owner any trouble?"

"Only once. Do you see that tall *hsiang-k'ung*, the second from your left? He is called Lu Su-lan. He's famous for his cleverness and his composure. But he was entrapped by the handcuffs, just like all the others. Instead of yelling, thrashing around and crying, however, he began to laugh, pretending to consider the thing a good joke. Then, when the Prince had undressed and begun to untie the prisoner's sash, Su-lan gave his would be attacker a well-placed kick in the groin and made him roll senseless to the floor.

"Then coolly and calmly he examined the mechanism and succeeded in releasing the spring with his teeth so that he could free his hands. He even had the audacity to drag over the unconscious Prince and clap his hands into the handcuffs. And, since there had been no noise to attract attention, he was able to walk out without any trouble."

"Before leaving," I asked, "did he at least impose upon the Prince the same torture that the Prince had destined for him?"

My neighbor gave a coarse guffaw, then shrugged, meaning he did not know. I continued my questioning.

"How is it that Su-lan is still alive after that?"

"Far from wanting to assassinate him, Li goes around boasting about his vanquisher's self-possession. And even sends him gifts from time to time."

"Poisoned cakes?"

"In any case Su-lan is still alive . . . furthermore he's more preoccupied by another of his suitors, Lan-tan. You must have heard of him? He owns most of the pawn shops in the Outer City. It's always a question whether his wealth exceeds his avarice or vice versa."

"A fat man, yellow, wry-faced with a wispy gray beard?"

"That's the one. Ugly as sin. And his First Wife berates him about his looks, which aggravates his humors, turning him into a mass of irritation, bitterness and fear of humiliation. One evening, then, he had himself announced at Su-lan's with a little friend, Chang, who detests him but follows him everywhere to take advantage of his money. They both entered without waiting for the *hsiang-k'ung's* answer.

"Su-lan, hiding his fury with dissembling smiles, treated them very well indeed, so well in fact that, under pretext of wanting to look at some old pawn tickets, he managed to get some given to him that are worth 300 ounces. Then he plied his visitors with drink until they fell down drunk. Servants undressed them and stretched them out on the couch. A man stayed with them, ready to serve them, while Su-lan went to sleep. In the middle of the night he is awakened by his servants. The fat Lan-tan, in his cups, lovelorn, totally unable to distinguish anything, had wrapped himself around his little sidekick and was murmuring honeyed words: 'My little Su-lan . . . my heart and liver . . . ' The *hsiang-k'ung* laughed until he cried at the spectacle, for Chang, overcome by wine, was totally unconscious of what was going on. After a while, however, the little man, no doubt sickened by the rhythmic movements, had some startling regurgitations. Then he woke up and tried to free himself from this heavy embrace. Being unable to, he turned on his attacker and began to threaten him. But at that precise moment the nauseating tide of his drunkenness welled up to his mouth and spouted from his lips, inundating the beefy Lothario. Lan-tan, who was by now suffocating and screaming, still did not desist from pressing his attentions. Finally Chang had to throw a punch over his shoulder, smacking him right in the face to make him let go. What infuriated Lan-tan most was finding out that he had been pursuing the wrong object."

"He must have been furious with Su-lan."

"Not at all. He only thought that the three hundred ounces of silver he gave the *hsiang-k'ung* were worth far more than Chang's love, poking or jabs. So he returned to Su-lan's in a few days, alone and ready to reproach him bitterly for having had himself replaced in that way. But Su-lan received him so graciously that the miser not only made no remonstrance, but offered him a solid gold bracelet worth at least two hundred *liang*. Nonetheless, this time Lan-tan decided not to leave without getting some attention. All alone the *hsiang-k'ung* was hardly in a position to refuse. Lan-tan was right at heaven's portal, if I dare express it in those terms."

"One must be tenacious in every endeavor," I interjected.

"Not so fast. At the last minute there's a clumping of heavy boots in the adjoining room. A servant flies in and warns in a hoarse stage whisper, 'It's the police . . . You must flee!' The fat man, choked though he was by lust, did not stop to ask if three times seven make twenty-one or twenty-two. He got up in a flash and flinging on his clothes helter-skelter he ran with Su-lan to the rear of the house where, with the aid of a stepladder and no little prodding, they succeeded in getting him out and down into the courtyard of the neighboring house. Needless to say the police had never entered the place at all. It was all a strategem prepared beforehand by the wily *hsiang-k'ung*."

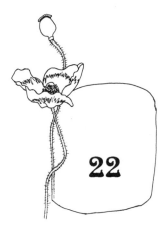

22

One May evening, in the season when heavy heat announced coming storms and summer deluge, I went to hear Pei Yu in a new role. Long before the curtain, the house had sold out. Around the pit and in the balcony, the aisles were full of standees so tightly packed they could hardly move.

In the audience one could already feel that nervousness, that yearning to admire and love that raises the sensitive and artistic souls of the singers and musicians above and beyond themselves, and calls forth an intensity of expression from them, a delicacy of nuance, a perfection that they can never find when separated from this mysterious element.

We were already anticipating the great artist's entrance and were astonished that the orchestra, after having called for attention with its overture of gongs and cymbals, did not proceed to charm our sensibilities with the melodious opening bars of the overture.

Suddenly a man in a blue robe, with a pale and tragic face, rushed on stage in place of the graceful silhouette we all awaited. In the deep silence that fell over the house, he cried out in an anguished voice:

"Gentlemen, a great misfortune has just befallen us. Pei Yu is dying!"

A deep gasp of horror went up in the house. The man lifted his hand and continued:

"Our Pei Yu, after being pursued and insulted by a man who lacks both modesty and principles, decided to end his life. He is already unconscious."

The entire audience, now on its feet, began to howl.

"Who is this miserable offender? Death to him! Let him be reincarnated as a dog or a pig!"

As the audience surged toward the stage, the door to my box was cleared. I profited from this circumstance and slipped away from the enraged crowd through the front exit, running to find my carriage still waiting for me where I had left it.

My poor mule, spurred by the whiplashes of the groom, who already knew the whole story, never trotted so fast in his life. Yet to me the time seemed interminable until we reached the missionary hospital, our first destination. I had no doubt as to the manner of suicide Pei Yu would choose and there would be only one method of saving him.

Impatience made my heart leap while I explained the case to the pharmacist and finally received from his indifferent hand an emetic and a hypodermic for caffeine injections, a prescription which daily saves many from suicide.

The gates of the Inner City were still open, and I was soon able to reach the Duck's Bill Crossing and the actor's house.

Once there what ravages met my gaze! The freshly painted door hung broken. In the courtyard I stepped over shards of porcelain and shreds of fine fabrics. Sculptured lattice-work, magnificent paintings, everything had been torn apart.

Wails of mourning guided my steps toward the bedroom where I found him, already seemingly beyond recall. The light of a red wax candle flickered over his outstretched, motionless body.

Kneeling in front of the divan, Chang the *shih fu* hammered the floor with his forehead and tore gashes in his face with nails. His ritual lamentation, however, was interspersed with moaning and groaning over his own fate. In common with all of us here on earth, he was not bemoaning the dead boy's fate, but, egotistically, his own loss. There was no one else with them in the devastated room. The terrified servants had all fled.

Without wasting precious time to verify if he were still breathing, I hastened to give him a caffeine injection. Then, under the anxious gaze of Chang, whose outcries I had interrupted by a well-placed kick, I picked up a fragment of broken mirror and held it in front of Pei Yu's lips. A slight mist formed there and almost immediately disappeared. He was still alive.

Soon, under the actions of the caffeine, his heartbeat, rendered sluggish by opium, began to grow more regular. The would-be suicide opened his eyes slightly and moaned softly. I immediately lifted his head and poured the emetic into his mouth. He swallowed it mechanically. It produced the desired effect: the danger was averted.

While vigorously massaging the poor, desperate boy to stimulate circulation and prevent a new heart failure, I had Chang tell me what he knew about the cause of this nearly catastrophic event.

Pei Yu had received a summons to dine at a restaurant, as is customary with those who want the company of a *hsiang-k'ung* but who also want to invite their friends to join them. This card however, belonged to Prince Li. Pei Yu refused immediately, pleading illness. On receiving this answer, Prince Li began shouting.

"Since when does a *hsiang-k'ung* dare to refuse when I summon him? I shall have him brought here by force, sick or well."

His guests somehow managed to calm him down. Apparently his gang of thugs were not with him at that moment, for matters went no further.

Several days passed and Chang thought that Li had forgotten his threats. But on that very day, just as Pei Yu was leaving for the theater, a new summons arrived from the Prince in the hands of a steward. The steward, on receiving a new refusal, immediately left the house and signaled the gang of hired thugs who had accompanied him.

The bodyguard had tried to defend Pei Yu with his cudgel, but to no avail. He only succeeded in cracking one skull, which enraged the attackers still more. During the commotion Pei Yu, terror-stricken, choked with rage and unable to flee, wrote out a hasty accusation against his persecutor, hid it on his person and then swallowed several opium pellets.

When the marauders finally forced open the door to his room, the poison had not yet taken effect, but the young man had begun to writhe around in frightful convulsions. The invaders, baffled by this, retired without touching him, but not before completely wrecking his room.

Chang was waiting for Pei Yu at the theater. Uneasy when he did not appear, Chang came to look for him. He found the house empty and silent and the child already unconscious, stretched out on the floor. There was one servant who, having been knocked out, was just coming around and could describe the whole scene to him. Then, doubtless out of fear that the attackers might return, he ran away on the pretext of going to look for help.

Meanwhile the sick boy began to grow more and more lucid. His initial lack of expression changed to animation when he recognized us. But when he looked around the devastated room a flood of tears took away the brightness of his gaze.

"Why did you call me back from the Land of the Shadows?" he finally moaned. "How can I go on living after such an insult?"

But a clear voice was heard in back of us:

"A sage said, 'The first duty of man is to combat injustice. The offended one must not think of death, but of exacting justice. Let him spare himself jealously for that purpose!'"

We had turned around anxiously. There at the door, his face contracted, eyes snapping, fists clenched, stood Star-of-Wisdom. He entered.

"As soon as I came in I realized that our benevolent genie had brought you back to life. My heart grew calm. But on hearing your words, I am choked with anger. Give me the complaint. I shall file it with the President of the Court of Imperial Censors at dawn and notify Minister Yüan."

Chang immediately drew the document he had found in the attempted suicide's garments out of his velvet boot. Pei Yu in a feeble voice sadly remarked:

"Do you really think the judges will hesitate for an instant between a Prince of the Blood and a little slave? It would take a paragon of virtue to do that and they are rare at any time. Why press charges? The Court will only throw them out."

Later we learned that Yüan, on reflection, advised against any denunciation. Prince Tuan's power was limitless and it was said that his own son had been appointed *T'ai Tzu*, Heir Apparent to the Throne, since the reigning Emperor lacked direct descendants. It would indeed be unwise to annoy Prince Li, who was his cousin. Once again at the clever old gentleman's suggestion it was deemed better to convert the whole affair into a scandal that would come to the Sovereign's ears. In evoking Pei Yu's first unsuccessful kidnaping we would heap endless ridicule on the noble Manchu's unfortunate and tenacious love and in this manner we could protect our friend from any fresh attempt.

Thus the tale, skillfully retold, excited the hilarity of all Peking. The Prince was characterized as out of his mind with amorous fury, smashing up everything in the hope of affecting the virtuous actor. Pei Yu's already spotless reputation was enhanced a hundredfold. He knew fresh artistic triumphs surpassing anything ever seen in living memory.

23

Pei Yu's glory, established henceforth, was confirmed each day by habitual outbursts of adulation from his fanatical followers. Parades, applause, gifts, poems: nothing was missing from his triumphs.

This glory, however, was not untainted and my simple occidental soul failed to understand how admirers, even the most passionate among them, could still fail to hide their ancient prejudices toward his state of slavery and toward his profession, which itself was still despised even while it had elevated him to fortune's pinnacle.

Therefore I was greatly surprised to read one morning in the *T'ing Pao*, the Capital Gazette, the text of a brief decree conferring on Pei Yu the noble Manchu title of *Bei-tzu*, which gave him the right to attend Imperial audiences without being called and conferred upon him the rare privilege of being able to touch the Sacred Body without incurring the death penalty as prescribed by the rites in such cases. At the same time he received the coral button, which gave him equal rank with provincial governors.

I hastened to him on horseback to present my congratulations and to learn the circumstances of this exceptional favor.

His porter, whom my groom called to open the narrow and recently repainted doorway, appeared with an air of self-importance. Recognizing me, he ran up gesticulating and saying, "His Excellency is detained at the Imperial Palace for ten days. He sends word that he'll be living there from now on."

In my stupefaction, I almost imitated my escort, who on receiving this news had widened his eyes in amazement and let his tongue hang out.

While we were slowly turning our horses around, the idea came to me that Chang the *shih fu* could doubtless give me some interesting details. He never failed, at the ritual feasts, to bring me gifts to prove his gratitude. This obliged me to maintain relations with him that were always criticized by my worthy majordomo.

Prudent and fearful, Pei Yu's fortunate master lived in a house of humble appearance, lost in a silent and calm quarter of the Outer City. Here I wandered a long time in solitude between two ancient walls whose tiles were overgrown with mosses and a plant known as Jupiter's Beard, wild grasses and sometimes ivy. At long intervals the walls rose in low gables or were separated by a narrow door with two stone steps. High above the bluish earth of the road, the weathered, brownish plaster of the walls, the gray tiles and the roof plants, there stretched the pale blue of a sky ever pure and light. Silence reigned, scarcely broken by the whistles attached to the tails of a few pigeons circling very high in the air.

Soon becoming lost and not daring to knock at strange doors, I noticed the humble, inconspicuous entrance of a small temple dedicated to the local deity, T'ou Ti, who watches our every action and informs the authorities of the Kingdom of the Shades so that everything may be entered into the registers kept for each immortal soul, across its successive existences. In the narrow courtyard paved with flagstones, jars of terracotta held a miniature forest of dwarfed trees. To the left, at the top of a few mossy steps, there stretched the long gallery where statues of the Three Spotless Ones stood and from whence there wafted the gentle fragrance of long joss sticking out of ashes held in antique bronzes. On the other side, the trellis of panels hung with paper was half open. I saw the priest and greeted him. He opened the door immediately, his face wrinkled with smiles, an old hermit living in solitude in the middle of an immense town. He knew the *shih fu's* house and took me to it.

It was an unpretentious house, made up of little courtyards with large flagstones. The rooftops were tiled in gray and were so low that

I could have touched them with my hands. The windowpanes held torn and blackened paper; the wretched rooms, once painted with whitewash, now had ceilings shiny with soot and walls covered with poetic inscriptions or comic drawings. Cheap furniture of heavy wood with broken crossbars whose colors had faded filled the rooms and a brick divan covered by tattered rush mats, the winter home of scorpions and vermin, stood against one wall.

Still, all the pavilions hummed with songs, laughter, cries full of young and joyous life. And in the waiting room where I was first led there was a reception line of young performers pushing and shoving to come and greet the "great man from overseas."

Their curiosity satisfied, their respects paid, one by one they returned to their interrupted rehearsal leaving me alone to muse over the lives of all these children. Not a single one of them could hope to catch the public's favor by virtue of beauty or talent. In order to tap the generosities of spectators who were more given to paying for bodily pleasures than for pleasures of the intellect, they were forced to struggle along while employing liveliness, gaiety and jesting tricks. A difficult and uncertain life where one who had known triumphs yesterday might today see his wittiest jests go unheeded, disdained.

Grown impatient with waiting, I questioned a servant. He admitted that they did not dare disturb Chang, who was crushed with grief. But at my insistence he took me to the back of the compound across a small garden of unusual flowers and strangely shaped rocks. There a luxuriously decorated room opened its doors of sculptured cedar.

In the splendor of this pavilion Chang had collapsed amid brocaded cushions, his face flushed scarlet, tears streaming from his swollen eyes. He held his head in his hands and uttered endless lamentations.

"Aya! Wu-hu! Alas!"

He finally became aware of my presence, shook his head as if in desperation and intoned lugubriously:

"Misfortune is upon me! I am ruined."

While patting his ample shoulder in commiseration, I questioned him. He replied:

"Elevation to the nobility freed him . . . and to think he used to bring me eight to ten *wan* a year!"

Once again he became racked by sobs. A *wan* was a weight of ten thousand ounces of silver, nearly three hundred and fifty kilos of metal. Ten *wan* actually made up a considerable revenue. I, however, objected:

"In the already numerous years that he has been pouring such a flood of money into your coffers, your treasure must have grown large enough to last to the end of your days."

"You forget that the teacher of Peking's leading singer was a power whom nobody dared disturb. Today I count for nothing; I can be attacked without fear."

"But he is more powerful than ever. One word from him will protect you from all attack."

"And then, a treasure that no longer grows is a treasure that diminishes. I loved watching my fortune grow from month to month."

Irritated by this avarice, I questioned him unsparingly. He spoke up, stopping frequently to sigh.

"Everything is the fault of that accursed Prince Li. The old Empress Dowager, she who holds the real power, quickly found out the meaning of Yüan's animosity toward Li. She interrogated Li, who was unable to hide his feelings. Only then did she order Pei Yu to the Palace, supposedly to organize theatrical performances, but in reality to amuse the Emperor who had fallen into melancholy and wanted to commit suicide."

"You don't mean to say that the Emperor—"

"I only know what I'm told. But I have not finished. Old Buddha herself was seized with curiosity to see Pei Yu. Whereupon she immediately withdrew him from the Emperor. . . I was in terror lest she have him poisoned or slaughtered as is her wont with many objects of her passing fancy. Instead she elevated him in rank. For me the results have been exactly the same. I am ruined."

And his moans were redoubled.

24

It was about that time that I had once again to leave the capital, with its sparkling northern sunshine, to go live in humid heat under Shanghai's cloudy skies. Once there, it took me some time before I could understand the sweet lisping dialect of the Lower Yang-Tse, so different from the clear, rough speech of Peking.

In the theaters it seemed as if I were in a strange country. The repertory was somewhat the same, but the style was totally different. The costumes were of more dazzling colors. The singers had a surprisingly nasal intonation. The orchestras did not attempt the same sonority or assonance as in the North. The rhythm was more marked, the harmonies were less agreeable.

And in Shanghai the *hsiang-k'ung* did not exist. Women's roles were played by young actors, but no one would ever dream of calling them to charm banquets with their wit and literary culture. To all such meals they invited the charming sing-song girls, the *kuan yins*, who, seated behind every guest, seduced them much more by dint of their gracious beauty, their pearl-laden coiffures and their necklaces than by the penetrating voices with which they interpreted their curious melodies to the accompaniment of guitar or tambourine. You had to insist if you wanted a theater song from one of them.

Dramatic art was not, as it was in Peking, the very soul of entertainment. Literature and poetry gave way to more immediate concerns. The wealthy businessmen of this opulent city, at the end of their

working day, only rarely attended theater. They preferred to gather in
brightly lit restaurants and linger over "guessing the fists," *chai chüan*,
a kind of betting game where you try to foretell the total number of
fingers extended or withheld as two players throw out their hands at
the same time, each one yelling what he thinks will be the figure
formed by his own contracted fingers as well as those of his adversary.

They talked more of business and politics than they did of poetry
or works of art. And they passed their evenings playing away fortunes
around the *ma-ch'üeh* tables, "sparrows in the hemp," which occidentals have come to know and call, for some inexplicable reason, mah
jong.

All along Foochow Road, the street of pleasure, rose the pierced
walls made of lacquered and gilded wood, the so-called *hsiu ch'ang*,
"arenas of literature," where the *kuan yins* arrived, carried by their
porters, to step now and then upon a dais to sing some piercing
melody for the pleasure of the tea drinkers who filled the hall.

We often heard them tell of the ruses of those women who were
trying to buy their way out of bondage, simulating true love in order to
be chosen as Second Wives. They would soon deceive, rob and
abandon their husbands to follow some vagabond who in turn would
rob them, beat them and leave them. They knew how to refuse
indefinitely to better excite desire and generosity. Then one night
while drunk they would give themselves to the first comer. They
knew nothing of the efforts made to achieve art and beauty, of the
incessant work of singers who cannot allow a day to go by without
practicing, without studying the poems of their repertory or new plays.

On my arrival, I immediately noticed the singular restlessness of
the town. Entire families, arriving from northern provinces, were

spreading rumors of the impending trouble that had driven them from their villages and made them seek the protection of the European fleets.

Throughout the whole center of the Empire, popular uprisings were breaking out against the foreigners and even against the natives. Bands of brigands were forming everywhere. The noticeable weakness of the authorities encouraged them to multiply their outrages. Ineffective leaders, agitated masses . . . anyone who was acquainted with the history of mankind could spot the preliminary symptoms of one of those fits of general madness which, from time to time, cause people to rise up—fits to which the highly-strung Children of Han are more susceptible than any other race. But if everyone in China and Europe could see this particular catastrophe coming, no one did a single thing to avert it.

Besides, in the Shanghai of those days, as at present, a distrust, a mutual aversion separated white and yellow, who would see one another for business reasons but never for pleasure. The occidentals even spoke with admiration of some amongst them who had lived for twenty years in the part of the city reserved only for Europeans without having ever visited the Chinese city whose black fortress walls nevertheless dominated their business district.

Thus, remote from China, although living there, I ceaselessly regretted being separated from my friends, the artists and scholars of the capital.

Therefore I was especially happy when one morning the press announced Pei Yu's arrival in Shanghai:

> *His Excellency the Bei Tzu, illustrious and incomparable enchanter, accompanied, like the sun with its planets, by a troupe of the best actors from Peking.*

An ambiguous article by the theatrical editor of the *Su-pao* aroused my curiosity. There were references couched in mysterious terms to a departure that was like a comet's trajectory, of the tears and blood of regret, of birds leaving a flaming bark and other still more obscure allusions.

Pei Yu was stopping, naturally, at the *Chi-sheng Chan*, "The Hotel of Favorable Advancement," an establishment praised by all Chinese visitors for its comfort as well as its excellent food. I especially liked it for its long inside courtyard, surrounded on all sides by a wide balcony of brightly painted wood connecting the rooms of the top floor.

This court, always lively with movement and gaiety, was on that day invaded by the curious come to admire celebrity. You could scarcely press through the jam. It was only with a thousand "*chieh kuangs*"—"I borrow your light"—and ten thousand smiles that I was finally able to reach the room where I was expected.

On the threshold where he greeted me, Pei Yu seemed to have matured. A man now, but ever graceful, undulating, strangely asexual. He offered me his hand, European style, avoiding both the kneeling that no longer befitted his rank and the genuflecting on one knee to the ground that is the customary sign of greeting between peers.

He led me at once to the divan and questioned me at length about myself and then about Shanghai; he was enchanted to know that I was the magistrate who would preside over any lawsuit of which he might be the object during his visit.

Then he went on to ask many questions about occidental military preparations and the possibility of sending troops to the North without delay. To such an extent that I exclaimed:

"Doesn't the Throne have the means of reproving the madness of the Fists of Harmony and Justice? Will it allow them to attack foreign property?"

He lowered his voice.

"The entire Throne trembles and totters. Prince Tuan has proclaimed his son heir to the Throne. He has promised the post and title of Protector of the Dynasty to General Tung Fu-hsiang, who has arrived by forced march from Turkestan with his brave Muslim army in the belief that the Eighteen Provinces will recognize Islam if foreigners are chased out of the Far East. Tuan expects to obtain either help or neutrality from troops armed in European style by Yuan Shih-k'ai. Then he will order the Empress Dowager killed together with the Emperor in order to place his son on the Throne."

"Will the southern provinces accept this change? What of the vice-realm of Hankow?"

"All China is waiting to see who will be her master. She only hopes that the struggle between the old and the new will cost her as little as possible in pillaging, murder, fire and famine. I remember now what was said by the elders of our village. 'Ah, how the slow-witted people would be rich and happy if they knew how to arm themselves and mercilessly kill all those who demand taxes or who want to trouble, even by a word, the profound tranquility of their labor!'"

"It is certain that if all the oppressed had the courage to massacre their oppressors, oppression would soon vanish from the earth. But the sheeplike multitude will always allow itself to be gulled by the lies of those who desire its fleece and its blood."

After a silence, I finally questioned my friend on more intimate subjects:

"Tell me something about yourself now. And tell me how the Chariots of Light brought themselves to the decision of allowing you to leave the Palace. Give me a detailed account of all that while also giving me news of your friend, Star-of-Wisdom."

At the name, his dark eyes grew melancholy. Without answering, he opened a fan he had been holding and showed it to me. On a white background a gifted painter had done a peach branch with carmine-colored flowers, tiny pale-green leaves that were hardly in leaf yet. Finally, he spoke, as if with regret:

"The blush of these petals were composed of drops of his blood."

"Is he dead?" I gasped. "Has he been assassinated?"

"No. No," he protested. "He is still alive since it was he himself who delicately added the peach blossoms to the rose-colored spots, the symbol of passion . . . "

Bemused I contemplated the object full of tragic mysticism while he continued:

"Before your departure from Peking you must have learned that the Dowager Empress' undisputed authority was beginning to diminish in the face of Prince Tuan's savage energy. A few months passed. Then little by little the Sovereign withdrew her special favor that was my only protection. I became apprehensive, thinking of the fate encountered by her former lovers and the mysterious demise of most of her favorites."

"Why shouldn't she allow you to leave . . . you managed it anyway?"

"The favorites know too much. It is wiser to be assured of their discretion."

"Was Star-of-Wisdom warned of your danger? His anguish must have been extreme?"

"He knew everything, since I saw him now and again with the complicity of the eunuchs. He announced himself as my musician and thus could enter the Palace under the pretext of bringing me new melodies and having me rehearse them. At that time he urged me to request permission to return to the theater. As for myself I hesitated, feeling that it would only signal my being put to death."

"Couldn't you find a way to escape?"

"You forget that in the Violet City where Imperial munificence had assigned me a pavilion in the gardens, three thousand eunuchs watch over the Sacred Body. No one can take a step without being seen and without having to account for his presence and his smallest move in a written report."

"What can one do in these circumstances?"

"Nothing. Wait for death."

"Still . . . "

"It was like this. One evening my friend and I, alone and closeted in my room, were discussing matters, anxious and troubled. Suddenly the door was pushed open brutally and Prince Li, the beast, entered. He had never known Star-of-Wisdom and spoke to me without paying any attention to him. He told me that at that moment Prince Tuan was making the Emperor sign an act of abdication. The Empress was renouncing all power and preparing to retire to a mountain convent. In addition she was tired of me and talked of having me poisoned. Thereupon Li told me that I had just one way of saving myself: I was to follow him docilely and give myself to him. Since his rank and station permitted him to move freely in the Forbidden City, he could cover me with his gold tablet and conduct me forth with no difficulty. . .

"You know that the Sovereigns grant a special tablet to pillars of the dynasty, so that they may control the guards at all times, and there is no one who, under pain of death, would dare defy them."

"What could you answer? You were forced to accept, to use cunning?"

"In my astonishment I didn't even have this thought. I was overwhelmed, speechless. He then produced a dagger from his robe and told me barbarously to choose between himself and immediate death."

"He did not see Star-of-Wisdom, who had slipped up behind him and who, in one movement, grabbed his arms, trying to disarm him and catch him off balance. The Prince was stronger than my poor friend. Even though surprised, he got out of it at once. Turning around he threw himself savagely on his aggressor with his dagger poised, ready to slice his throat open. Now beside myself, I remembered what he had done that night when I barely escaped his clutches. I snatched up an antique bronze and tried to deal him a violent blow on the skull from behind. He heard me, turned around and ducked to get out of the way. A sharp corner of the heavy object struck him on the temple. He crumpled to the floor."

"Dead?"

"So we assumed. Star-of-Wisdom, pale and out of breath, went to get a woven scarf from the table to bind up his wrist that had been cut open. Some drops of his blood rained onto the white silk of this fan where a few moments before he had been composing a poem. Now he would be forced to flee at all costs. While he took possession of our victim's weapon and golden tablet, all I could think of was saving the fan that had been stained by his precious blood."

He was silent for a moment, doubtless reliving those violent moments. I broke the silence at last:

"No one disturbed you as you left the Violet City?"

"The Prince's tablet opened every door. We went immediately to my former master, Chang, since we had nowhere to hide, no clothes and no money. Chang, fearful of being utterly ruined by my flight, bent himself to the task in such a manner that scarcely two hours later we were leaving the Capital with all our luggage. A few kilometers from the city wall, the train welcomed us into its palatial apartments and, rolling on its two metal rails, carried us as far as Tientsin in the time it takes to let out a shriek. We were saved."

I then expressed the pleasure I would find in greeting Star-of-Wisdom. Pei Yu's face grew dark again.

"I didn't tell you the whole story. At Tientsin, in the hotel where we hid out before our intended departure, travelers arriving from Peking after us told us that by order of Prince Li absolutely everyone who wanted to pass the gates had to be inspected. A proclamation had been publicly displayed everywhere promising a thousand ounces of gold to whoever could bring me before the Prince 'whom I had tried to assassinate, daring to shed blood within the Sacred Precincts of the Violet City Itself.' Star-of-Wisdom, learning in this way that Li was still alive, decided to leave me despite all my entreaties. He has sworn to avenge us. I would have gone along with him if my face had not been so well known that it would have spelled certain disaster for the enterprise. Since then I have not received a single word of his whereabouts."

26

Insanity, true mistress of mankind, had triumphed once more. The outside world, having no news from its diplomats, immediately thought that all of its Peking representatives had been massacred. A blockade and siege of the diplomatic quarter had, in fact, begun. All foreigners and Chinese converts in the northern provinces were arrested, tortured and put to death. The foreign powers united in order to punish this common affront . . . most of all to stop one another from annexing too much territory.

At Shanghai, while the youth of the city went on parade organized as voluntary militia, barracks were being hastily prepared to receive the regiments of all races who were streaming ashore from Indonesia, Hong Kong, Indo-China, the Philippines, America, Japan and Siberia.

Every language could be heard on the lawns of the Bund, where at nightfall during the summer the citizens have the habit of coming to enjoy the relatively fresh breeze blowing over the yellow water of the Whangpoo river and to hear the municipal orchestra, which is accompanied by the incessant chirring of crickets from the trees.

The river was already crowded with ships loaded with refugees. There were large, flat river junks from the Grand Canal and Nanking. From the high seas came tall and medieval-looking vessels with immense anchor eyes in their bows and bridges like citadels astern. Long courier ships came from Europe and imposing clippers from

America.

All the old steamers that had been put into mothballs were hastily put back into service, transporting provisions for armadas concentrated in the Gulf of Pechihli or to bring south frightened northern refugees.

In this manner the population increased daily, and the houses built in haste for the new arrivals formed new suburbs bigger than the old town. The entire city grew prosperous from feeding these countless mouths.

In spite of, or perhaps because of, an uncertain future, this fever of activity, of movement and of work was also a fever of pleasure. Existing shops grew larger. Restaurants sprang up everywhere and the gaming houses were never empty.

The corpulent *shih fu* Chang had not let such an opportunity to add to his fortunes go by. Within two months he had built a theater that was larger and handsomer than any in town.

He called it *Hsin Wu T'ai*, "The New Terrace of Dances." He raised the prices four or five times what was being asked elsewhere; nevertheless the house was always full. Chang had, indeed, been very careful to guarantee every single performance with Pei Yu, whose immense renown constantly drew fresh crowds of spectators.

Chang, it must be admitted, paid his former slave a monthly stipend that outdid anything the most rapacious viceroys managed to squeeze from their dominions. And for the "free" performances, for theater parties that the powerful businessmen gave in their association houses, their *hui-kuan*, Pei Yu received up to a thousand ounces of silver before even granting the favor of his presence.

And while Shanghai grew stupefied with pleasure, riches and liberty, in the North there were more and more ruins. Villages were depopulated; fields lay neglected, bereft of autumn sowing.

The Allies bombarded and took the forts at Taku, occupying the coast and disembarking their troops. A march to the interior was organized. Tientsin, under fire from Chinese armies, became the rallying point for the armed forces. Finally, a column of a thousand men tried to get to Peking.

But the column was forced to fall back before the numerous troops who held the countryside. In holding back the Allied forces,

The Fists of Justice and Harmony thought they had won out over the entire world.

27

One day Pei Yu sent word for me to come and see him in the house he had rented on an island in the large canal that passed near the town, in the countryside half asleep in the humid heat.

I found him in a cool room that opened onto masses of flowers in a garden bordered by a large expanse of tranquil water studded with pink lotus. At his side he had a man with a gaunt face and burning, frightened eyes. I recognized him at once: it was Star-of-Wisdom.

As soon as he saw me he threw himself on his knees and struck his forehead on the thick carpet. Surprised, I immediately drew him up with ritual phrases. Then, seeing that he could not get hold of himself, I added:

"Ten thousand good wishes, O Ancestor! Deign to inform me how I may help you, I beg you."

Almost fainting, he remained kneeling without saying a word. Pei Yu, with my help, made him sit down, and said:

"He implores your protection . . . We both have great need of it."

It was necessary, as usual, to make many digressions in order to obtain a detailed account of the facts.

Star-of-Wisdom, after having left his friend at the moment when the latter left Tientsin for Shanghai, had wanted to return to Peking. He looked around for a cabdriver, but no one wanted to take him there. All the boatmen refused to go back up the river. No one wanted to risk life and possessions by going anywhere near the ravaged capital.

Several days went by in this way, full of fruitless attempts.

Discouraged, he left alone, on foot. He hid during the day among the reeds on the edge of Pei-ho river. At sunset he silently approached the deserted villages, going through the houses to try to find a few provisions that the troops and the looters might have left behind.

The Allies, at that time, had not yet landed on the coast, whose protective forts were considered unassailable. The movement of troops against the enemy was scarcely beginning. The traveler could thus cover the greater part of the road without running into trouble.

Near the town of Tungchow he left the Pei-ho and followed the Jade Canal. There were no longer any reeds among which to hide nor even any bushes in this country of vegetable garden cultivation. The villages were more numerous and still in part inhabited. He was forced to hide in barns and stables.

Not far from the capital, while breaking into an empty house where he hoped to find a little food, he saw an officer of the Yuan Shih-k'ai Army stretched out on the ground with his throat cut. While rummaging through the rooms, the thought came to the young man that, in time of trouble, an officer's uniform makes everyone flee: looters, military or not, who fear having to share their plunder, and those who have already been robbed and fear to lose still more. It is a passport that safeguards anyone from being rudely questioned for fear of immediate reprisals.

He thereupon stripped the corpse and appropriated his effects. In his pockets he found orders and papers in the name of a certain Wei, a battalion chief; thus his identity itself was assured. He proceeded openly from there on. He stopped the first wagon that crossed his path, filled with baggage, seized the horse's bridle, and at gun point had himself driven to within view of the somber, medieval walls of Peking.

Seated at the side of a ditch, he scrutinized the deep archway of the city gate. How could he get through? The project seemed hopeless, for Boxer guards and turbaned Moslems filled the opening, searching all travelers brutally.

A troop of soldiers finally passed on their way to the city. The false officer risked following them, slipping in among them in the archway's shadow. No one questioned him. He boldly passed within the walls.

Within the high walls there was smoke and fire on all sides. Cannon and gunfire could be heard near the diplomatic quarters, and isolated gunfire could also be heard all over town. Soldiers everywhere were pillaging the houses, and from all directions came the anguished screams of women or of young girls, or the screams of men being tortured to oblige them to reveal their hidden treasure.

Star-of-Wisdom feared arrest at any moment. He was overjoyed to see that, on the contrary, everybody kept out of his way. Wasn't he, as an officer, a leader of the murderous pillagers? He determined to watch over the movements of Prince Li so that he might devise a means of putting him to death. With this in mind he went to the noble Manchu's palace.

The door was shut. Silence reigned within. No guard was on duty before the portico. He wanted to question the neighbors and knocked on the first shuttered door he found. Obtaining no response, he knocked more persistently. Without opening they asked him from the interior what he wanted. He learned that the Prince had already sent his family and his treasures far from the city under safe conduct. He himself with his eldest son remained behind since they were both obliged to appear at the Palace every day. And when the false officer expressed surprise at the absence of a guard, the neighbors laughed. From what would one of the main Boxer leaders need protecting? Did he not have the sacred insignia nailed over his door?

An idea immediately flashed into Star-of-Wisdom's mind. He tore down the Boxer's insignia from the portico. Then he ran toward the center of the town and harangued the first band of looters that he met, jeering at them for wasting time on houses of the poor when the palace and treasures of a Christian prince were standing unguarded.

Respectful of his rank, the looters believed him unquestioningly. They forced a panel of the outside door and invaded the inner courtyards. A servant tried to resist. He fell with his skull split wide open. Others, surprised, allowed the crowd of aggressors to pass, so they reached the Cinnabar court straightaway.

There on marble steps leading to the main hall were the Prince and his son, surrounded by a few determined men. Forewarned, they had had time to take up their sabers and they seemed bent on making a desperate resistance.

There was a moment of hesitation in the attack. Bellowing and cursing, the soldiers brandished their weapons but did not dare to advance. Two of them who had loaded rifles took aim badly, fired but wounded no one. However, the attack had made the defenders draw back slightly, leaving in the forefront the Prince and his son, who had not moved.

Then one of the looters moved away from his companions, cast a big net over the two Manchus and pulled them to the floor where, powerless, they continued to struggle and bellow. A determined charge from the aggressors terrified the servants, who were already demoralized by the capture of their master, and they ran away.

Immediately the looters, fearing the arrival of reinforcements, bound the arms and legs of their captives, ripped off their clothes and attached them facing one another to the columns of the veranda.

Then a soldier armed with an evil knife seized the boy's white arm, squeezed a piece of his flesh and, ready to slash, turned his head toward the father, addressing him ferociously:

"Where are your treasures?"

"Gone," said the Manchu curtly.

"You lie!"

And a large piece of flesh fell to the ground. A dog, appearing suddenly from nowhere, pounced on the bleeding gobbet and carried it off. The father started forward so suddenly that the entire column shook. His bonds tightened, cutting into his own flesh. He bellowed imprecations. But what could he do? His treasures were really gone.

Hacked apart bit by bit, the son was soon nothing more than a bleeding pulp. His head finally slumped onto his chest. He breathed his last.

The father's face, convulsed with hatred, had such a terrible expression that the soldiers were frozen and hesitated to touch him. Star-of-Wisdom then grabbed a broken wooden stake and dashed out the eyes of the tortured victim.

The looters, their nerve returning, began the interrogation once again, punctuating each question with some new torture whose atrociousness sometimes made them laugh nervously. But the Prince was long beyond replying.

Then the false officer cried into his ear:

"Do you remember all those you insulted and mistreated during your miserably long life? Do you remember Pei Yu? Your crimes have aroused mysterious forces. At last you die and your present tortures are as voluptuous caresses compared to the endless agonies you will undergo in the Kingdom of the Shades!"

28

Extraordinary events followed one another in such rapid succession in the North, and we were informed of what transpired in such a haphazard manner, that the imaginations of both occidental and Chinese journalists could run riot. At one time we were assured that Tuan had massacred the entire royal family and proclaimed himself founder of a new dynasty. On another day it was announced that the Dowager Empress was about to marry the Mikado.

But the Chinese journalists frequently published authentic documents which had some interest. In particular the reports and decrees appearing in the *T'ing Pao*, the Palace Gazette, which still appeared fairly frequently, carried reports given by governors on their provinces. Local revolts were described in such a way as to give no opinion for or against the Fists of Justice. So their power remained uncertain.

One day I read with surprise and anxiety a violent report signed by my old friend Minister Yüan and also by one of the Imperial Censors, Hsü Ch'ing-Ch'êng. It is known that the Censors form a legal body, charged with apprehending and bringing to justice all crime, iniquity and immorality in the Empire, be the criminal the Emperor Himself. And their actions are even more infallible since they themselves may be charged before the Minister of Punishments, the Minister of Rites and a member of the Privy Council for any weakness or partiality shown in their mission, for not denouncing a crime as well as for having been mistaken in denouncing it. This responsibility was great enough and capable of provoking such scandals, that the Court was obliged for its own security to choose only persons of sound character.

Yüan and Hsü's report was dated the twentieth of June, just after the first attack on the diplomats. After the opening formalities they had written:

> . . . Since the sixteenth of this moon, the Fists of Justice have been in the capital as invaders. The Throne, afflicted by the calamities that have befallen the Flowery Kingdom, has held audience each dawn seeking the advice of its humble Councilors in order to save the Ancestral Temples and the nation itself . . .

> And nevertheless since the twentieth day of the moon, the Fists of Justice have been able, without any interference of any kind, to set fire to more than a thousand dwellings around Ch'ien Men. So effective have they been that this quarter, once the richest of the city, is nothing more than a hideous desert. Nine-tenths of the capital's inhabitants have fled. Purveyors of food and money no longer reach us from the provinces. Words cannot describe the desolation, suffering, and misery of the people.

> In conclusion it is written in the Records of the Rites of Chou: "When disorder ravages the State, it is imperative to apply the death penalty unreservedly to all those guilty." In the Classic of Prose it is also written, "There are, alas! periods when infliction of the supreme penalty becomes a sacred duty." It seems proved that the hour has arrived to exterminate the fomenters of disorder. Any indulgence or delay will bring about frightful disaster. Humbly we submit this request and we implore Your Divine Wisdom to come to a rapid decision.

No action followed these sage counsels. Some time later I saw a second report, bearing the same signatures and dated the eighth of July. The audacity of the Minister, at the very hour when the Boxers seemed to be masters in the Palace, surprised me. The adroitness of the old courtier had not prepared me for this boldness, for this violent and direct attack on his enemies. And this action was all the more hazardous, given that he and his friends were doubtless suspected of having engineered the death of Prince Li. For it is difficult to keep an act under cover, and, as the old proverb has it, the only way to keep an action hidden from everyone is not to commit it. Nevertheless the daring accusers had written:

Since the twenty-fourth of the moon, when the Fists of Justice murdered the German ambassador, they have held the diplomats under siege. Now suddenly troops commanded by General Tung-Fu-hsiang have joined them to make the unfortunate inhabitants of the capital suffer the maximum through the merciless looting of their homes. That disbanded troops and hordes of brigands should thus be openly authorized by the Throne to ravage the capital is a unique occurrence in all our history. . .

And the military value of these brigands is nil. They first boasted of razing the diplomatic quarters in twenty-four hours. But in a whole month they have barely succeeded in killing a few foreign soldiers, whereas thousands of their own corpses strew the approaches to the besieged area. How can the Throne place confidence in them to defend us against the foreign armies who at this moment are landing on our shores?

As K'ung Tzu ordered, the Throne has just sent presents to the diplomats in order to testify to Its good will towards those who come from afar. At the same time the Fists of Justice continue their attacks. If the foreigners should infer from this that the Sacred Throne is being hypocritical, how will It be able to prove Its innocence and Its disapproval of the massacres?

On the other hand, the foreign powers claim that they are sending their troops in order to suppress the rebellion and to re-establish order. Of course such declarations strain our credulity to the breaking point. Would it not be better, however, to crush the rebels ourselves, in order to rob the foreigners of any pretext for intervention?

Alas! The Clear Light of Heaven is temporarily obscured by the pestilential invasion of destructive locusts. We are absolutely certain that our overly sincere remonstrances will be our undoing. But, our humility notwithstanding, we feel strongly that China is like a dying man whose every sigh may be his last. The fear of speaking weighs less heavily on us than does the sense of duty.

Knowing that we face death with our audacity we nevertheless address this memorial to the Throne, begging It to draw inspiration therefrom, and to act.

To my great surprise, the newspapers mentioned neither the execution nor even the arrest of Yüan and Hsü. Was Tuan losing influence? Did the Empress hesitate to sacrifice those who might be able to support her against the indomitable Boxers?

Two weeks later, on the twenty-third of July, the *T'ing Pao* published another report, or violent denunciation rather, signed by Yüan and Hsü:

This is a memorial, whose objective is to point out humbly that the Sacred Capital is ravaged by anarchy; that the whole Empire is laid waste by brigands; that we are on the eve of war with the entire Universe. The outcome of this can only be an unprecedented catastrophe.

In centuries past, if there were sometimes rebellions of extreme gravity, the Throne and the people at least proclaimed that the fomenters of disorder were nothing but rebels. But today those closest the Throne call the Fists of Justice "fervent patriots" and use such terms that no one dare call them rebels. These bandits, when beginning their movement, adopted the motto: "Sustain the Dynasty and destroy the foreigner." Would it not be wise to remember this? Those who are strong enough to sustain are strong enough to overthrow. The danger is grave.

It is, therefore, not only on the heads of the rebels themselves that the just wrath of the Throne should fall, but also on all those, be they the highest in the land, who in their folly have supported and encouraged the Fists of Justice. Their relationship to the Throne can in no way excuse them from punishment for their faults.

In this way the foreigners will be convinced of the uprightness and loyalty of the Throne. In this way the rumblings of war will be transformed into peaceful conversations. In this way the Ancestral Temples will remain inviolate.

And when the Goddess of Mercy has rolled the heads of bandits and criminals, even those closest to the Throne, may She order our execution as well, so that our death may appease the spirits of those great ones who are guilty. We shall cheerfully go to our death.

We submit this Memorial in an irresistible movement of indignation and alarm. We anxiously implore the Court to act.

Four days later a curt note announced that Minister Yüan and Censor Hsü had, on orders of the Sovereign, been arrested and taken to the Ministry of Punishments. There, no trial, as demanded by Imperial Law, was held, but a simple reading of the decree ordering that they be put to death.

A long time afterwards Pei Yu had me read a note on yellow paper folded in book size as is customary for mourning.

Written by Yüan's eldest son, it had been sent to all the members of his family, to be filed in the archives and transmitted to his descendants. Pei Yu had received it as "adopted son" of the Minister.

I found therein the account of the circumstances that led to Yüan's glorious condemnation, as well as the detailed description of his final moments.

When the old man, under arrest, had been led to the Ministry of Punishments, he knew already what would happen. He donned his Court robes and all his insignia of office. In the Honor Hall of the Ministry, a table had been prepared, covered with yellow silk embroidered with five-clawed dragons. The decree scroll lay there between two lighted candelabra. Hsü, dressed similarly, was already present.

The Minister of Punishments, also in court dress, knelt on one side of the table; Yüan and Hsü on the other. Then all three had struck their foreheads to the ground nine times as if in the Sovereign's presence. Then the Minister, still kneeling, had unrolled the decree covered with a large Imperial Seal and had solemnly read it aloud. The three officials had then prostrated themselved nine more time to thank Heaven for having manifested Itself in such a way.

Then Yüan had said calmly to his old friend who was lamenting his fate:

"Things had come to such a pass that even had I remained silent I should have been forced to flee or perish. I prefer to give myself to the executioner that my death might cause the Throne and the nation to reflect, to convince them of the dangers risked by their weakness and inaction. Thus I die content."

His children, who had been sent in, had gathered around him moaning and crying. He reproved them in a kindly way:

"I give my life to try to save my country. Be proud of the honor that fate assigns our family. It is the greatest that a servant of the state may obtain."

And thus he spent the night, chatting and laughing, surrounded by his loved ones.

The next day at one o'clock in the afternoon, Yüan and Hsü, both clothed in their court robes embroidered with the insignia of their rank, were led to the execution ground followed by the executioner, who flourished a large saber.

The site was packed with Fists of Justice, a dense and hostile crowd. As the fatal procession slowly approached, one of the rebel chiefs placed himself in Yüan's way and furiously demanded why he had always struggled against the true patriots. The old gentleman had shrugged his shoulders gently and answered:

"Do your comrades believe that their ignorance and folly are on a par with the reason and loyal sentiments of a scholar? Do they then dare to compare themselves to high magistrates?"

A few steps farther on the executioner made a rapid pass with his steely weapon. Yüan's head rolled on the ground. A fountain of blood poured from his neck. His body vibrated, then fell heavily. Right beside him the Censor was also decapitated while upright and walking.

Those who kneel before the Sacred Person may never die kneeling before the executioner's aides.

29

Toward the end of the month of August, I learned with astonishment that Pei Yu, breaking all his engagements, had suddenly left Shanghai and sailed for the North. When I questioned the *shih fu* Chang about this departure he seemed to know nothing beyond infinite regret at losing the future gains that he'd counted on.

Could Pei Yu be thinking of taking up his triumphant career in Peking once again? But theaters in ruined cities generally do not reopen for a long time and, even if he did sing, it would be to a decimated and impoverished public. He could never find the same success and money that he knew daily in opulent Shanghai. I could not understand his thoughts.

For me another question also remained insoluble: When they had entered Peking, why had the Allies not quickly occupied the Gates of the Forbidden City? Their strange hesitation had permitted the entire Court to escape and reach the open countryside. And even at that moment a swift squadron might have arrested the procession, which had barely left town, and prevented them from taking refuge some two thousand kilometers away in ancient Changan, capital of the Han and T'ang dynasties. Why had nothing been done?

I was to remain ignorant of the reasons for these two inexplicable actions for quite some time.

A few weeks later I was sent to Peking myself. The situation there was as strange as could be imagined. The entire Chinese gov-

ernment was now out of any danger, first of all because of its distant
location, second because the Allies distrusted one another so thoroughly. They had not, for a considerable length of time and despite
their equal desire to expand, been able to reach any agreement as to the
partitioning of China into spheres of commercial and industrial influence. Would one army simply allow the others to conquer their own
regions? On the other hand, the certainty of not being able to come to
an agreement after the conquest of China by an interallied army, rendered a joint expedition undesirable since it would be as costly as it
was useless.

The northern population had willingly favored the Fists of Justice
when a hope existed of joining in the pillaging of foreign establishments. But the North had rapidly tired of seeing itself, on the contrary, pillaged and decimated by the so-called patriots. The North was
now welcoming the foreigners as saviors, all the more since all taxation was suspended, and material and moral liberty had never been so
great, even though order was being strictly maintained. A few Manchu
families, out of loyalty, closed their doors jealously to the conquerors.
Otherwise everyone was vying with everyone else for favor, full of
smiles and affability, sending out invitations and exchanging friendly
visits with officers and soldiers of the Allied armies.

As I had suspected, theaters had not yet opened their doors.
Most of them had been gutted by fire and had not been rebuilt. The
companies had been disbanded. Many of the *hsiang-k'ung* had acquired freedom by running away.

It took me several days to discover Pei Yu's new residence. And
I only found it because Chang, having given up all attempts at exploit-
ing Shanghai without a star, had returned to Peking himself and had
taken good care to call on me in order to assure himself the protection
of the provisional masters of the capital.

Pei Yu was living under the purple ramparts of the Forbidden
City in the ungutted part of a former Manchu palace that dated back to
the Conquest.

In the immense hall whose lacquers were faded by time, splendid
furniture and thick carpets were still intact. The art objects and hanging scrolls had disappeared, removed either by the fleeing owners or

by successive looters. But no one had been able to destroy entirely what refined generations had left there of nobility and delicacy.

If, upon entering, I was struck by this atmosphere where the gracious silhouette of Pei Yu moved very naturally, guiding me to the depths of the room, I received a very real shock when I perceived, in the shadow of a divan enclosure with open-work carvings, a recumbent man dressed in a European uniform bending over a tray of opium.

The smoker, suddenly seeing an occidental, got up. I was all the more troubled, for I recognized one of the most distinguished officers in the Allied command, distinguished by his present situation as well as by the scandal of which he had been the principal figure in Europe the year before. His photograph was still fresh in my mind since it showed him stripped for action and holding on his lap a little second lieutenant who was also down to the buff.

What was he doing here with Pei Yu? And what about Pei Yu, the artist who was only devoted to music and literature, and the friend of Star-of-Wisdom? What did he want of this foreigner?

The stiff and formal visitor finally withdrew. My host, after seeing him to the door, returned to sit by me. Our conversation began again. But while our idle words flew back and forth softly in the heavy silence of the ancient chamber, our thoughts remained secretive and seemed to be trying to read one another silently.

What weighty secret was he hesitating to reveal?

He must have finally perceived the bitter conjectures that were jostling one another in my troubled spirit, for he gave a long sigh. Then, pushing away the tray that separated us, he leaned toward me and said in a whisper:

"I find the silent hostility of your suspicions insufferably offensive. I beg you to come out with what you find inexplicable or incorrect in my conduct. You were astonished to see me leave Shanghai so quickly when the Allies entered Peking? Then why did they, who were supposedly putting down the Boxers to re-establish order, do nothing to arrest and punish Prince Tuan, their principal leader? Don't you think that once he was arrested, tried and beheaded, all Boxer resistance would have ended at once and justice would have been done for all the crimes he instigated?"

Why hadn't they attempted to capture the Court while it was still easy for them to block the Four Gateways to the Forbidden City?

But none of these questions explained his sudden departure. Why really had he come to Peking? He continued:

"I thought that the Allies were either deceived by Japan, who is only too glad to be left alone with a permanently divided China, or else that they were ignorant and incapable of acting, as is usual with mutually jealous associates, and that they were going to allow Prince Tuan to become Emperor."

Then changing his expression to one of extraordinary hatred, Pei Yu continued: "And since Prince Tuan is the man who had my benefactor executed, I do not want him to become Emperor. I would rather see him live a long time while plunged in opprobrium and degradation, so that the growing suffering of his thwarted ambition might be for him a longer and more bitter punishment than death itself."

"How do you hope to be able to influence Allied decisions?" I asked, surprised.

"I had no set plan, and furthermore no illusions about the difficulty of obtaining my desire. But we of the East are not beset by the notion that we can direct events. We know, on the contrary, that events make use of us. Our decisions are always dictated by what our past, our milieu and circumstances impose on us. My will to act, having had a cause, could not therefore lack an effect. As soon as I arrived in Peking, I began searching for a way to influence the Commander-in-Chief of the Allied Forces."

"Your appearance alone could easily turn the head of the Manchu lady who occupies first place in the Commander's heart. And through her, despite her lack of influence and her probable ignorance of politics—"

"How can you speak words so utterly lacking in common sense? You know our people and history. And since women are alike everywhere, you must have observed in your own country what cunning your friends' wives use in order to influence their husbands' plans and decisions. You ought to know that the Manchu woman was adroitly cast into the Commander's path through the machinations of Prince Ch'ing shortly after he returned to Peking with the Empress' secret instructions. But Ch'ing is still not sure whether Prince Tuan might not be appointed Regent tomorrow. That's the reason he pretends to support him."

Actually I had been surprised to note that the Allied Council no longer placed Tuan's punishment among the first conditions of the Peace Treaty, whose terms had been drafted while awaiting for the Court to make negotiation offers.

I asked thoughtfully: "How then win over a man blinded by the love of women?"

"Since his judgment was overruled by his feelings, I needed to find another means of influencing his decisions. I suddenly thought of the principle established by Wu Tzu two thousand years ago. 'A military chieftain knows life only through the reports of his aides.'

"Ah!" I sighed with relief, "That's why you made friends with his Chief of Staff."

Pei Yu gave me a happy smile.

"I saw very well that you refused to believe in a situation that seemed unfavorable to me. But your inner certainty was shaken by the evidence before your eyes."

A short while later, to the Allies' great surprise, the Empress appointed a pure Chinese, the elderly Li Hung-chang, as Minister, giving him full power to negotiate a peace. The Manchus were ignored. At the same time all the Chinese dailies spread word that Tuan's death was demanded by the foreigners under pain of a permanent occupation of China.

The entire country, still vacillating between two powers and two political points of view, was so moved by the Empress' decree that countless requests were addressed to her imploring her to return to Peking and conclude peace.

On the following day I chatted with Pei Yu and expressed my astonishment at such a bold decision on the part of the Empress; above all, I was astonished that even from Changan, 500 miles from Peking, she should be so well-informed as to the exact moment when her move would simultaneously paralyze Prince Tuan, return the people's blind confidence to the Throne and sway the Allies in her favor.

He smiled at me with an amused look. Then without answering he took me by the hand and led me to his chamber.

A single scroll was hanging on the walls of pale green lacquer. He showed it to me. The picture showed a rocky gorge in which a river's rapids boiled. An old fisherman was drawing out his line whereon hung a small carp. Very high and to the left, written with a firm and strong hand that I thought I recognized, were the words: "A little fish can prevent a man's dying of hunger." There was also a large vermilion seal that I could make out at once. The hand was indeed that of the redoubtable Empress. There was also a date. The painting had been sent scarcely a fortnight ago.

I wheeled around in surprise and conjecture. He placed a finger to his lips and smiled, saying:

"Our beloved Empress, the Old Fô, has always said that a wise Sovereign ought to know how to utilize the talents of her most humble subjects."

And I murmured, while inwardly admiring the fine and able flexibility of Asia:

"Ten thousand congratulations on the return of Imperial Favor."

30

The people of Peking, while awaiting the return of their former masters, enjoyed a freedom they had never known before. Displaced persons, now reassured, returned in great numbers. With work and life, business and wealth began to grow again in the capital, and the people set about rapidly to repair its ruins.

Pleasure seemed the principle occupation of the inhabitants— every imaginable pleasure, to judge from the song and laughter that rang out night and day in the entertainment quarter, the *Lou-li-ch'ang*, which now covered the entire northwest of the Outer City.

Modesty and morality no longer placed any restrictions on sexual fantasies. It even seemed that these satisfactions were more intense for being displayed in public. Freed by the great upheaval from the artificial bonds imposed for centuries by religious or Imperial shepherds whose only concern had been to squeeze profit from their human flock, this humanity regained its equilibrium and returned at once to free and joyous Nature. Forgetful of a past that nothing could bring back, heedless of a future that no one could predict, people gave themselves up unreservedly to every joy they could experience.

And those who profit from supplying pleasure to the seekers found it an easy matter to make a fortune. The *shih fu* Chang, who showed me from time to time a gratitude that was not unmingled with an expectation of future benefits, spoke with pride and satisfaction of the way he was handling his assets.

A group of foreigners to whom I mentioned by chance the

various businesses of the crafty *shih fu* immediately insisted on visiting establishments that were unknown in Europe. Their interest, purely scientific according to them, finally extracted from me the promise they desired.

That same evening, Chang, fat, smiling, dressed in his best figured-silk robe, guided us through his holdings. First of all, his *hsiang-k'ung* restaurants. He owned a whole street of them. They were mainly houses hastily rebuilt of clay mixed with chalk and straw, with a coat of plaster, white on the inside, iron gray on the exterior. Modest furnishings lacquered vermilion filled each room: tables, chairs and wide divans. From court to court, from room to room everything looked like everything else. And all of it was full of people drinking, eating, singing, served by shady-looking chaps who appeared ready to commit any crime.

Children made up in vivid hues, dressed in long pale robes, languorously circulating, caressed in passing by the drinkers, were finally embraced and pulled down on the knees of customers who were soon escorting them to the back room. And the breeze caused by their movement flung aside the children's unfastened garments, revealing their scrawny limbs.

A house served as a school for the neophytes. When asked where they came from, since it was not likely that an irresistible vocation had drawn them, Chang made an equivocal reply. The poor little ones, supposedly sold by parents who could no longer feed them, were more probably collected from ruined villages or stolen from the streets of neighboring towns. The *shih fu* pointed out proudly that the instructor's zeal never slackened and that studies were pursued very late into the night—classes in voice, deportment and diction were still in full swing.

Noticing that Chang was leading the procession of the curious away from a room where infantile voices could be heard, I remained behind and softly pushed the door open. I heard the master inquiring:

"By what do you recognize that a customer will waste your time and as a consequence rob your master?"

Several voices answered together:

"He will offer us neither food nor drink! He will only try to paw us."

"How does a *hsiang-k'ung* help a customer to rob his master in the fastest way?"

"By not insisting that the customer pay in advance . . . "

The children, seated on benches, had their garments spread around them and remained motionless. This surprising immobility came to an end suddenly on the professor's signal. All the children arose.

What on earth were those pointed sticks of graduated size on which they had been squatting?

Chang returned with the visitors, who followed the direction of my gaze and immediately began to exclaim in surprise and amazement. The *shih fu*, irritated, said as if to excuse himself:

"Well, it just has to be done progressively. Things would be too difficult otherwise; the customers would shy off . . . "

There was a total silence amongst the curious. That evening we went no further.

A few days later, Chang, being asked again, led his visitors into a neighboring street that also belonged to him and that the Greeks would have dedicated to Aphrodite. But the excessively ugly women who showed their bizarre make-up at every doorway were the cause of visible disappointment. And when we asked him if he had nothing better to show us, he seemed thoroughly humiliated and let us a little way farther on.

Through the door and we were in a large courtyard surrounded by handsome buildings, shaded by old trees. The porter, recognizing his master, gave a call. From the main hall there came running and jostling one another a bevy of budding girls. The youngest seemed to be five years old. The oldest could not have been even ten.

Several of the visitors were no longer young; their eyes began to sparkle. Chang suddenly became nervous and cried out in a tone of supplication:

"Take it easy! Gentlemen, please! Take it easy!"

Having remained in the court, under the twinkling (and perhaps lewd?) star-filled sky, I could not help letting my gaze be drawn toward the torn-paper panels of a chamber where glowed a lantern bedecked with peonies.

One of our ranking gray-haired companions of the Allied Armies was in there, standing half-nude, before the bed. With both hands, he had hold of the legs of a little girl stretched out before him . . .

I will never forget the red face of that man, puffing and sweating, whose pince-nez was trembling and ready to fall off. No less will I forget the young girl's silent tears, her eyes lifted in mute supplication towards Heaven where is said to reside He without Whose express order no straw may be moved.

Chang returned to join me. He could feel my silent judgment and to excuse himself told me that the success of his "dry daughters" was greater with the foreign troops than with the city's inhabitants.

Undoubtedly the adventure became known, for the following Sunday the chaplain of the Allied Army made it the text of his sermon. But he knew he cried out in vain by citing scripture, by menacing his flock and all Peking with the same fate the Almighty dealt Sodom and Gomorrah. The foreigners themselves, released from the artificial restrictions of their laws and of their educations, obeyed once more all the instincts, all the desires that their Creator had placed in their immortal souls and continued (as their pastor styled it) "to wallow in the filth of their own lechery."

A licentious giddiness was indeed suddenly pervading foreign get-togethers. A new game became the rage. One of Chang's children would hide under a table with the duty of "servicing" one of the guests seated around it. All of guests were to remain alert, watching one another, ready to pick up the slightest sign of emotion that might betray the passive recipient, who, once discovered, had to get up immediately and, making his weakness known, promise the winners some costly invitation.

When springtime arrived, it was not unusual to see coolies in tatters prodded into mimicry by the sight of a couple of dogs in heat. Laughing and joking they would throw themselves on all fours and, right there in the street, emulate the sex-crazed animals.

For more than a year this went on. Peking was thought of as a paradise of freedom.

Then the peace treaty was finally signed. Prince Tuan, foremost of the great criminals, was condemned to death, stripped of his rank and privilege, but at the last moment his sentence was commuted to life imprisonment. Thus Minister Yüan was avenged.

The Dowager Empress, rid of the Boxers and their chief, thanks to those same foreigners she had once ordered blasted off the face of the earth, returned to Peking and reclaimed all her power.

Pei Yu, now a Duke of the fourth rank, was named permanent director of the Imperial Theater and received the carved coral button. The Yüan family made him a solemn gift of the same gardens where for so long he had been the Minister's guest.

31

... A sharp pain in my finger cast me brutally back into the present to the warm comfort of my English armchair. The cigaret that I had lighted—was it twenty years ago?—had burned slowly, until it burned my hand ... In those few moments our mutual past had filed in review before my eyes.

Pei Yu, not the young man of yesteryear, but the grown man of today, had completed his sentence without having noticed my absence. Besides, hadn't I been there all along?

"Since the Revolution of 1911, fortunately for me, our epoch admires the artist above all. My photograph is in all the shop windows beside that of the Chief of State. I earn more than all the ministers put together and am given more honors than a viceroy in his own province. Destiny is favorable."

"May it heap you with ever-increasing favor!" I said.

I stood up and joined hands for an amicable greeting, while I added:

"It must be getting close to your performance time. Permit me to withdraw from your company."

"Today won't you give me the pleasure of singing especially for you? We are giving an opera you used to like very much, 'A Soul Returns to Peony Pavilion.'"

"You do me a very great honor. You know the joy that I always find in listening to you."

The light of his smile illuminated his face, just as the glow of a
meteor lights for an instant the dark night. We descended from the
high chamber and crossed the gardens in the brilliant sunshine that
banishes all care and memory.

In the portico a heavy limousine was idling, awaiting our departure. After wrapping myself in furs, I notice that there was a footman
seated beside the driver and that standing on the running board there
were men hanging from straps posted in front of each door, each with
one hand on the heavy revolver in his belt.

These precautions were surprising but Asian politeness forbids
questioning; therefore I remained silent. Still, the thought came to me
almost immediately that if the town's lack of security necessitated such
an armed force, the thin walls of the automobile would hardly stop a
bullet coming from behind.

My looks and expression must have betrayed my thoughts, for
my companion remarked simply:

"It's armor-plated. That has to be done now. The jealous stop at
nothing."

We approached the high gray wall that you must pass in order to
leave the Inner City. The driver doubled his speed and suddenly made
a left into the tunnel. My neighbor murmured:

"From the top of the wall a bomb could easily be tossed . . ."

Then he smiled again and recited the beginning of a *jaoling*, a
tongue-twister carefully composed so that the least error of accentua-
tion or enunciation changes its meaning and gives an unexpected and
scandalous connotation. In days gone by, when six or seven of us
were packed into my car going to dinner nearby, we thought we would
die laughing at the errors that we all used to make.

We had already left the Ch'ien-Mên's wide outside avenue to
enter the Ta-chia-lan. The rasping squawks of our horn were redoubled. The crowd grew thicker and thicker. We were surrounded
by pedestrians and cabs in every form, from the little rented open
rickshaw to the closed coupe drawn by a swift runner and furnished
with dazzling acetylene lamps.

Large horse-drawn carriages passed, full of laughing women,
jewels sparkling on the bright silks of their tight jackets. Automobile

horns rent the air. The coolies cried out ceaselessly, trying to open up the road. These sharper noises were sounded over a continous background of laughter, calls and jokes. It was truly the "warm racket" so dear to the Chinese heart.

In front of the walk leading to the theater a dense crowd was jabbering, quietly being held in order by the black and white striped silhouettes of police guards with fixed bayonets.

When our car arrived there was a moment of silence, then acclamations. The crowd pressed so tightly around us that the police running up were forced to rap the feet of gawkers with their rifle-butts to make them draw back, so we could get out.

They could not, however, stop one charming, elegantly dressed young woman whose precious stones glittered under the brilliance of the arc lamp. She threw herself at my friend and, clasping him in her arms, rapidly gushed some passionate phrases, reproaching him his coldness and begging for a rendezvous.

He tried to disengage himself, but in vain. In the laughing crowd, pleasantries began to rain on the "spring woman" and the "jade man." Pei Yu had to call on his footmen to help him get free.

Finally we were able to advance, passing the public entrance and skirting along the smooth wall of gray brick until we had pushed open the stage door and entered the theater.

He guided me affectionately by the hand, amused by my astonishment at the changes that had taken effect in the old place, which I had not seen for so many years . . . years during which I had lived in the silence of a little mountain town in the extreme southwest of the Empire where both theaters and restaurants were unknown; where the duties of my post took me off on long journeys on horseback, over the high hills, across valleys carpeted as soon as springtime came with opium poppies that made a covering of crimson or silver in the matchless, uncertain light.

The vast greenroom of yesteryear that had surged with life and gaiety was now cut up with low partitions and doors of inexpensive wood. Each of the actors had his own dressing room. The foyer behind the two openings that led to the stage was now only a lonely corridor.

While Pei Yu was changing, I went, following the old custom, to look at the audience through the gap in the "marshall's exit," where the spectators see the actors come on stage from their left. Indeed it is not very smart to look out from the opposite end of the stage through the "general's re-entry," because the doorway is often pushed open violently for a rapid exit from the stage.

Gongs, cymbals and drums, as in other times, were already beating the overture with great rhythmical strokes, announcing the beginning of the play.

What a transformation there was in the hall! Rows of armchairs now faced the orchestra instead of the seats and square low tables that had filled the lower floor, and on the balcony that ran along three sides of the theater there were also seats, and not a single table! The entire right side of the balcony was filled with women, most of them covered in jewels. Under the wings, too, women were mixed with men. What a change!

I felt someone pull my sleeve. It was Pei Yu in a long, feminine robe, his eyes lengthened with eyeshadow, his head covered with a chignon decked with flowers. I indicated the beauties seated in the balcony and asked:

"So is it permitted now?"

He shrugged his shoulders and said:

"All our traditions are crumbling. And the female spectators don't care much if an actor has talent. They only appreciate his beauty and want him to be masculine, even in feminine roles. We have theaters where only women perform. Their stinging jibes at the *hsiang-k'ung* neutralize the men's enthusiasm. The refinements of our mores have disappeared. Even for the banquets now they often import the seductive sing-song girls from the southern regions—from Yangchow and Soochow. Their nasal songs have the charm of being exotic. Their gentle flattery attracts the coarse and superficial tastes of those who govern us and grow fat on us today. The charms of their bodies make you forget the emptiness of their intellects and the fickleness of their hearts. . . When will the slime of materialism that sullies the world sink back to the bottom of the well, leaving clear and transparent once more the pure waters of intellectual delicacy and grace of feeling?"

We were interrupted. Violins were beginning the prelude. It was his entrance. With one leap he cleared the doorway. Then he advanced with little steps, all the while balancing lightly as if on mutilated feet. The entire audience broke out in "Hao! Hao!" and as quickly hushed again. The pure and harmonious voice of my friend welled forth in a flood of crystalline sound.

I hastened around to the front of the theater to get into the audience and listen to the play.

On the wide stage, before a drop representing a garden of giant, multi-colored flowers, the young beauty, sleeping amid the peonies on a warm spring afternoon, lived again a dream of love with the transparent soul of a young scholar who was also asleep very far from there.

I was really very fond of this Sixteenth Century work, which had crowned its author, T'ang Hsien-tsu, with endless glory and which was performed every year by one or another of the theaters in the capital.

The poetry of ideas and sweetness of music in the first duet of the two enamored souls soon swept one away, far from painful reality. Then came the moving death scene of the young girl, feverish with love and begging to be buried under the peonies, witness to her passion. Finally, the arrival of the young scholar, who recognizes the garden, the pavilion and the flowers where in the springtime past he had lived a dream of love whose perfection had rendered him insensible to all of life's seductions.

The shade of the young girl then appears at the edge of the lake under the fragrant trees and orders her lover to take her out of the grave and call her back to life. The heavy coffin is opened. Her body is discovered intact and she awakens to her lover's passionate caresses.

When feeling touches us not—is not our soul asleep within us as if in the depths of the grave? Is not each new love like a true resurrection?

Pei Yu animated this ghost with a mysterious and overwhelming life. Maturity, far from having removed the powers or the freshness of his voice, gave him accents of passion that enthralled everyone in the audience. He had that complete power over the deepest part of our psyche which only the greatest artists possess.

May he keep his talent to the ripest old age.

George Soulié de Morant

George Soulié de Morant had the height and bearing, high cheek bones, luminous, piercing, slightly almond-shaped eyes of a Native American. Even in the presence of his only son, Nevile who resembled him amazingly, one might have detected the spirit guide of a Plains Indian, or a Karankawa of east Texas. Indeed, his mother, Blanche Bienvenu de Vince was an American whose family had been settled in Louisiana since earliest times. Her ancestors may well have intermarried with descendants of those ancient *coureurs de bois* who often took Indian wives.

When George was seven, his father, an army engineer was lost at sea en route to joining Ferdinand de Lesseps, then breaking ground for the Panama Canal. Blanche took charge, placing little George in the College des Jésuites and later the Lycée Condorcet. He was said to have found them both intolerably stifling, but he nevertheless developed some excellent study habits and his intellect blossomed.

At 19, he arrived at the beach resort of St. Enogat in Brittany. There he fell under the spell of the exotically beautiful Judith Gautier, daughter of poet Théophile Gautier and singer Ernesta Grisi. Judith, already 40, was a bluestocking and an orientalist trained by a Chinese scholar Tin Tun Ling. This ex-member of the Han Lin had somehow managed to get stranded in Paris after the collapse of the Taiping Rebellion in 1865. Théophile had added him to the household.

The meeting of Judith and George seems to have produced one of those highly charged intellectual passions. She taught him Mandarin and launched his career in Sinology.

Within a year of finishing military service, Soulié de Morant was off for Shanghai. Speaking and writing Mandarin fluently, he became secretary-interpreter of the Chinese Railway Association. The Boxer Rebellion had recently been quelled, and cholera was ravaging the country. During the epidemic, Soulié de Morant witnessed some extraordinary cures effected through acupuncture, and he became vitally interested in this ancient form of therapy.

Next named as interpreter at the French Consulate in Shanghai, a double career in diplomacy and ethnology opened for him. He served as judge of a joint tribunal in Shanghai before being sent to posts in Hankow and Yunnan-fu (today's Kunming). At Yunnan-fu in particular, where he was one of very few resident Europeans, he once again had occasion to observe extraordinary cures effected by acupuncture at the local hospital. Thanks to the friendship of the Viceroy who gave him access to an immense library, he was able to amass important documentation in Chinese on the subject, material that he would reveal to the West in 1930.

Returning to France at the beginning of the Chinese Republic in 1911, Soulié de Morant married, established a family, and began to pursue his literary activities in tandem with his diplomatic career, all the while writing books and articles on China without a pause. Although malaria, contracted in the Far East, kept him from active military duty in the War of 1914, in 1917 he was sent back to China by the Minister of Public Instruction with the support of the Minister of Foreign Affairs. According to the orders of this mission he was charged with "preparing, through investigation and research, a French Center of Archeological and Artistic Research and Study comparable to the ones already existing in Athens and Cairo."

This mission lasted almost a year, during which time his family received practically no news of him. With his linguistic virtuosity (he knew Mongolian as well as several major dialects) he could easily have disguised himself to travel the length and breadth of China incognito. But why? Mystery still enshrouds this mission. It would be his last voyage to China, where he had spent about twelve years all told.

After World War I, he turned more exclusively to a literary career. For ten years, novels, translations and adaptations from Chinese, articles on China, on her art and theater poured forth exhaustively. To this period exactly belongs our novel. Soulié de Morant also wrote and lectured extensively on Chinese acupuncture and is considered one of the first to bring this Chinese art to the Western World. George Soulié de Morant died in 1955 at the age of 77.

G.F.

Glossary

"Aya! Wu-Hu!" - General interjections expressing annoyance, grievance, lament.

Beileh - Conventional transliteration for the title of Duke of the third rank of Manchu Princes.

Bei-tzu - A Duke of the fourth rank of Manchu Princes.

Boxers - The last days of the Manchu dynasty were troubled by a great impetus to modernization led by a group of scholars and educators from Kwantung and by foreign powers who had established major spheres of influence throughout China. By 1895, they had gained sway over the unusually bright Boy Emperor and were carefully grooming him to step out of the feudal past. The Dowager Empress, acting as regent, lacked confidence in the security of the Manchu powerbase (their popularity had always been questionable). Leaning on the "Fists of Justice" led by the mystical rabble-rouser Prince Tuan, she contrived the discovery of a plot against the throne and squelched the alleged sedition with a violent public upheaval. The Boy Emperor soon died conveniently and mysteriously, and was substituted by the more tractable Henry Pu-yi, child of another concubine. Of course, the Empress was deceived as to Tuan's loyalty and support. The whole maneuver backfired. Peking was sacked and burned, the Forbidden City besieged. The Empress found herself fleeing the capital on foot disguised as an old peasant woman.

The Bund - An artifical dike, embankment, dam or causeway. In the Anglo-Chinese ports the term was generically applied to the embanked quay along the shore. The term is specifically applied to the grand esplanade along the Whangpoo river in Shanghai where rose the European concessions and the modern city with high rise and apartment buildings.

Chao Fei-yen - Died 6 B.C. Daughter of a musician named Fêng Wan-chin, she was trained as a dancing girl; her grace and lightness were such that she received the name of Fei-yen, "Flying Swallow." At her father's death, she and her sister Ho-tê took the surname of Chao and found their way to the capital. There she was seen in 18 B.C. by the Emporor Ch'êng Ti, when his Majesty was roaming the city in disguise. The two girls were forthwith placed in the Imperial Seraglio, and Fei Yen became a favorite concubine to the exclusion of the famous Pan Chieh-yü. In 16 B.C. she was raised to the rank of Empress Consort, Ho-tê being honored with the title of Lady of Honor, but on the death of the Emperor she was driven by palace intrigues to commit suicide.

Changan - Now Sian, capital of Shensi province, and one of the ancient capitals of China.

Chieh Kuang - "I borrow your light," i.e., "by your leave."

Ch'ien - A copper coin, a tenth of a tael.

Chin - Traditional transliteration. The Chinese pound or catty. One and one-third English.

Ch'ing, Prince (1836-1916) - I-K'uang. Grandson of Yung-lin (1766-1820), first Prince Ch'ing. I-K'uang made Ch'ing in 1884. Raised to Prince of the First Degree in 1894, but with negligible power until after the Boxer War. When the court fled Peking in 1900, he also fled to Hsüan Hua, but on August 26th he was ordered to return to Peking to cooperate with Li Hung-chang. After he and Li signed the Protocol in 1901 ending the hostilities of the Boxer War, he contined to conduct foreign affairs. In 1903 after the death of Jung-Lu, he was given the highest offical position in the Empire. From 1903 to 1911 he served as Chief Grand Councilor, and from May to November 1911 he held the rank of Premier.

Chi-sheng Chan - Famous hotel of Shanghai circa 1900.

Classic of Prose - Also known as the Classic of Documents, attributed to Confucius.

Fô, Old - In Peking, "Fô" means Buddha. The term was sometimes used to describe the Empress Dowager (see Tzu Hsi).

Forbidden City - The inner city of Peking, where the imperial court resided.

Hao - Good.

Hsiang-k'ung - Young male performers, often portraying females. It is generally accepted that they owed their origin to the fact that the mother of the Chien L'ung Emperor had been a palace actress. She was said to have been embarassed by this fact and thus decided to have all women permanently barred from the stage. She may have also been quick to notice her son's coldness towards females. It is said that Chien L'ung's First Wife felt so humiliated by his constant neglect that she took a nun's vows and retired to a Taoist convent for the rest of her days. After the fall of the Manchus and the advent of the Kuomintang the days of the *hsiang-k'ung* were numbered. They were formally abolished by government decree in 1913.

Hsiao Fang-niu - Literally "Imitation of Pastoral Life." A popular and anonymous work having great vogue around the turn of the century and up until the Kuomintang.

Hsiao-shêng - Young gentlemen.

Hsi-Wang-Mu - The Fairy Queen, one of two rulers among the immortals. Hsi-Wang-Mu reigns over all female genii.

Hsiu Ch'ang - "Arenas of literature." Also may carry the connotation of "bawdy house."

Hsü Ch'ing Ch'êng (1845-1900) - Sometime Minister of Berlin, put to death by T'zu Hsi for his outspoken criticism of government policy during the Boxer War.

Huang Ti - The Yellow Emperor (2698 B.C.).

Hua-chêng-tan - "Flappers." Ornamental actresses.

Hua Tan - Actress.

I-Ho Ch'üan - Fists of Harmony & Justice (i.e., the Boxers).

Jih Pao - Daily News.

Ju Pao - Evening News.

K'ang - Has two meanings: 1. a stove bed; 2. the divan in a guest room.

K'ang-chieh, Tai-chieh - Literally, "repose step, great step."

K'an Pei - To remember with gratitude.

King of Liang - Sixth century A.D. The King of Liang lost 15,000 men from his own army when he involved them in a plan to inundate an enemy city by building a giant dam that would break. The scheme backfired when the dam broke prematurely.

K'o T'ou - Commonly transliterated as "Kowtow," a ceremonial bow in which one touches the forehead to the ground.

Kuan Yin - The Goddess of Mercy, worshipped in China before the advent of Buddhism and adopted by Buddhists as the female incarnation of the boddhisattva Avalokiteshvara. (See Tzu Hsi.)

K'un-Ch'iang - Earliest known Chinese operatic style.

K'ung Tzu - K'ung Fu Tzu, or Confucius.

Lao Tzu - (Sixth Century B.C.) Most respected of Taoist scholars and author of the *Tao Te Ching*.

Lao-Yeh - "Sir" A term of respect.

Li, Prince - Probably Shih To; senior of the eight Iron-capped Princes, being a descendant of Tai Shan, the second son of Norhachu; was on the Grand Council for some years.

Liang - A tael.

Ma-Ch'üeh - Mah jong, literally "sparrows in the grass," a parlor game still played today around the world.

Manchu - Name given to the ruling class of the Ching dynasty. Racially derived from Manchurian and Buriat stock, they seized control of the capital from the Ming Dynasty in 1644. They remained in power until 1912. Under the vigorous emperors K'ang Hsi and Chien L'ung, they expanded the Chinese Empire to greater size than it actually is today. At their best, they fostered and preserved Chinese letters and culture. At their worst, they were cruel, repressive and censored everything that criticized them in the slightest degree. The power of the dynasty found itself severely crippled after the Second Opium War.

Meng-Tse - (Mencius) a Chinese philosopher of the Third Century B.C.

Mi-Tzu - Probably Mo Tzu, also known as Mo Ti, who lived between 500 and 396 B.C. His doctrines include Universal Love.

Pang-Tzu - An ancient operatic style. Also, a musical instrument, i.e., a clapper used as a time beater.

Pao-Pei - Cowrie-shells, used as a medium of exchange. Many words with the general significance of "value" in Chinese are based on "pei," which originally meant a cowrie-shell. The cowrie is a molusk (Cypraea moneta).

Rites of Chou - Celebrated classic by Confucius.

Shih Fu - "Teacher."

"A Soul Returns to Peony Pavilion." - *Mu Tan T'ing Roa Roun Tsi,* a renowned classic play of the late Ming dynasty. See *T'ang Hsien-tsu..*

Ta-Chia-Lan - A district in Old Peking containing many theaters and restaurants.

Tai Shan - Holy Mountain of the East. West Central Shantung. Long revered by both Taoists and Buddhists.

T'ang Hsien-tsu (1550-1616) - The author of Mu Tan T'ing.

T'ao-Li-T'ien - Paradise. Literally, the Heaven of Peaches and Plums.

Theocritus - A Greek poet born in Syracuse ca. 270 B.C. The fragment given is the second half of his Idyll XII, known as "The Two Friends."

T'ou Ti - A local deity of Peking.

Tuan, Prince (Tsai-I) - Sponsors of the Boxers. Gained ascendancy over the Empress Dowager and was in control of Peking when the legations were under siege.

Tu Fu - (712-770 A.D.) - Famed poet of the T'ang Dynasty. Considered by many to be the greatest of all the Chinese poets.

Tung Fu Hsiang, General (1839-1908) - Around 1895 became commander of an army sponsored by Jung-Lu. The Kansu Braves, consisting of 10,000 men, mostly Mohammedans. They were openly anti-foreign, and on June 11, 1900, they murdered a secretary of the Japanese legation. Later Tung's soldiers in Peking joined the Boxers in pillaging, burning and murdering. General Tung was deprived of all rank and office.

Tzu Hsi (1835-1908) - The Dowager Empress, last ruler of the Manchu Dynasty. She rose from a concubine; self taught, she was a scholar with talent in both art and calligraphy. (See Boxers.)

Yang-Ti - Probably Yang Chu (c.440-360 B.C.), whose doctrines have been misinterpreted to stand for hedonism and egoism.

Yüan Ch'ang (1846-1900) - Native of Chekiang, decapitated in 1900. Sometime Minister to Berlin. Put to death by Tzu Hsi for "foreign proclivities."

Yuan Shih-K'ai (1859-1916) - Late in 1899, he was sent to Shantung as governor. He suppressed the rising tide of Boxers in that province and thus forced them northward into Chihli where they won official approval and brought on the Boxer War of 1900. During the war Yuan maintained order in Shantung and expanded his army to 20,000 men. On March 10, 1912, he became successor to Sun-Yat-Sen as President of the Provisional Government of the Republic.

Wu Tzu - The Emperor Wu, founder of Chou.

Note on Transliteration

In the mid-1970's I was working on a glossary for *Pei Yu* at the Orientalia Division of the Library of Congress in Washington, D.C. I had become aware of the complexity of the overlay of Chinese transliteration found in the work, and was seeking to clarify and simplify it, to get some kind of uniformity. Soulié de Morant as a Sinologist certainly availed himself of the transliteration system known in France, the EFEO, Ecole Française de l'Extrême Orient, as well as some traditional usages which predated either EFEO or Wade-Giles.

Suddenly in 1975 everything had become Pinyin. Peking (Beijing) had so ordained. Pinyin, the newest form, was also the oldest—the Portuguese Jesuits of Macao developed it in the Seventeenth Century. However, since Pinyin was not used at the time of Soulié de Morant, this translator has received almost universal counsel to stick with the older forms like traditional and Wade-Giles. This is to say that our transliterations are unabashedly lacking in uniformity.

In addition, we have pruned drastically whatever we could and very frequently used translation where the author had repeated his transliterations. All of this was to assure greater clarity and readability.

—The Translator

References Consulted

China Under the Empress Dowager. J.O.P. Brand and E. Backhouse. London: William Heineman, 1911.

The Chinese Drama from the Earliest Times until Today. Lewis Charles Arlington. Shanghai: Kelly & Walsh, 1930, re-issued 1966.

Chinese Literature: A Historical Introduction. Ch'en Shou-yi. Taiwan: Shin Yueh Publishing, 1978.

Chinese-English Dictionary of Modern Usage. Lin Yutang. The Chinese University of Hong Kong, 1972.

The Classical Theatre of China. A.C. Scott. London: George Allen & Unwin, 1957.

The Dictionary of Philosophy. Dagobert D. Runes. New York: Philosophical Library. No date.

Eminent Chinese of the Ch'ing Period. Hummel. Two volumes. Washington DC: the U.S. Library of Congress Orientalia Division, U.S. Government Printing Office, 1943.

Famous Chinese Plays. L.C. Arlington and Harold Action. New York: Russell & Russell, 1963.

The Five Thousand Dictionary: A Chinese-English Pocket Dictionary and Index to the Character Cards. Fifth edition. Cambridge, MA: Harvard Univ., 1940.

Guide to Transliterated Chinese in the Modern Peking Dialect, I & II. Ireneus László Legeza. Leiden: E.J. Brill, 1969.

An Introduction to Chinese Literature. Liu Wu-Chi. Bloomington, IN: University Press, 1966.

A Mandarin-Romanized Dictionary of Chinese. MacGillivray. Third Edition. Shanghai: Presbyterian Mission Press, 1911.

Passions of the Cut Sleeve: The Male Homosexual Tradition in China. Bret Hinsch. Berkeley & Los Angeles: University of California Press, 1990.

Science and Civilisation in China. Joseph Needham. (Volume I, Introductory Orientations). Cambridge: Harvard University Press, 1961.

Theater East and West: Perspectives Toward a Total Theater. Leonard Cabell Pronko. Berkeley and Los Angeles: University of California Press, 1967.

A Treasury of Chinese Literature: A New Prose Anthology. Ch'u Chai and Winberg Chai. New York: Appleton-Century, 1965.

H/50